Justify Me

Also from J. Kenner

The Stark Trilogy:
Release Me
Claim Me
Complete Me
Anchor Me
Lost With Me (coming Oct. 2018)

Stark Ever After:
Take Me
Have Me
Play My Game
Seduce Me
Unwrap Me
Deepest Kiss
Entice Me
Hold Me
Please Me (coming August 2018)

Stark International
Steele Trilogy:
Say My Name
On My Knees
Under My Skin
Take My Dare (novella, includes bonus short story: Steal My Heart)

Jamie & Ryan Novellas:
Tame Me
Tempt Me

Dallas & Jane (S.I.N. Trilogy):
Dirtiest Secret
Hottest Mess
Sweetest Taboo

Most Wanted:
Wanted
Heated
Ignited

Justify Me
By J. Kenner

A Stark International/Masters and Mercenaries Novella

Introduction by Lexi Blake

EVIL EYE
CONCEPTS

Justify Me
A Stark International/Masters and Mercenaries Novella
Copyright 2018 J. Kenner
ISBN: 978-1-945920-76-9

Published by Evil Eye Concepts, Incorporated

Sign up for the 1001 Dark Nights Newsletter
and be entered to win a Tiffany Lock necklace.

There's a contest every quarter!

Go to www.1001DarkNights.com to subscribe.

As a bonus, all subscribers will receive a free copy of
Discovery Bundle Three
Featuring stories by
Sidney Bristol, Darcy Burke, T. Gephart
Stacey Kennedy, Adriana Locke
JB Salsbury, and Erika Wilde

An Introduction to the Lexi Blake Crossover Collection

Who doesn't love a crossover? I know that for me there's always been something magical about two fictional words blending and meeting in a totally unexpected way. For years the only medium that has truly done it well and often is comic books. Superman vs. Batman in a fight to the finish. Marvel's Infinite Universe. There's something about two crazy worlds coming together that almost makes them feel more real. Like there's this brilliant universe filled with fictional characters and they can meet and talk, and sometimes they can fall in love.

I'm a geek. I go a little crazy when Thor meets up with Iron Man or The Flash and Arrow team up.

So why wouldn't we do it in Romanceland?

There are ways out there. A writer can write in another author's world, giving you her take on it. There's some brilliant fanfiction out there, but I wanted something different. I wanted to take my time and gradually introduce these characters from other worlds, bring you in slowly so you don't even realize what I'm doing. So you think this is McKay-Taggart, nothing odd here. Except there is…

Over the course of my last three books—Love Another Day, At Your Service, and Nobody Does It Better—I introduced you to five new characters and five new and brilliant worlds. If I've done my job, you'll know and love these characters—sisters from another mister, brothers from another mother.

So grab a glass of wine and welcome to the Lexi Blake Crossover Collection.

Love,

Lexi

Available now!

Acknowledgments from the Author

A huge thank you to Lexi for letting me play in her world, and to Liz, and MJ for letting me enter the playground in the first place!

Prologue

I should never have let him get close, this man who swept into my life like living flame, beautifully wild and dangerously enticing.

Didn't I know the risks? The price?

Wasn't my soul already bruised and battered?

And yet he slipped through my defenses and edged close to my heart.

Now I'm balancing on a precipice, and all I can do is hope that, despite everything, he'll catch me if I fall.

Chapter One

Riley Blade reeled back as the frog-faced man's surprisingly strong punch landed soundly against his jaw, snapping Riley's head back and pissing him off.

This, he thought. *This was why he'd sworn to stay the fuck away from Los Angeles.*

And yet here he was again, risking bullets and bruises when he could be downing a Scotch in one of the many bars that dotted the international terminal at LAX.

Clearly, he needed to have his head examined.

Then again, he thought as Froggy took another swing, maybe he should take the punch and see if it knocked some sense into him.

Since that option sounded more painful than practical, he shifted left to avoid the impact, swung his own arm up in a maneuver designed to both deflect and detain, then grabbed Froggy's wrist and twisted the wiry punk around. By the time Froggy started to howl, Riley had him in a headlock.

"I warned you not to hit me," he growled, to which Froggy replied with a heartfelt, though not very inventive, "Fuck you."

"Not my type," he said amiably, then spoke to the security team listening to the conversation through the hot mic and earpiece Riley wore. "All done. You wanna come relieve me of this piece of shit?"

"Good work, Blade. On my way." Less than fifteen seconds later, Ryan Hunter stepped in, tall and lean, and looking every bit the badass. The dark-haired security chief for the multi-billion-dollar Stark conglomerate and Riley went way back. Although Hunter had always been private sector, their paths had crossed multiple times during Riley's days in LA as an FBI SWAT team member, and they'd become good friends, often mistaken for brothers because of their similar build and coloring.

They'd kept in touch even after Riley escaped from La-La Land, and it was that tug of friendship that had landed Riley in this cheap motel room that stank of sex, urine, and something else that Riley really didn't want to think about.

"Appreciate the assist," Hunter said. "I've been knee deep in assholes for the last few days. A little conversation with this one should go a long way to rounding up a few more and clearing my workload." He flashed a wicked grin at Riley. "Which means Jamie thanks you, too," he said, referring to his wife. "She gets cranky when my nights are spent without her. Especially if I'm in a motel."

If what Riley remembered about the stunning brunette was accurate, she was more of a Ritz-Carlton girl than a No-Tell Motel type. But he understood where Hunter was coming from. Not, however, from personal experience. Riley's nights had always been his own, and if there was a woman in his bed beside him, there was no expectation on either of their parts that she'd still be there the next night.

For years, that had been the way Riley rolled. Lately, though, he'd been spending too much time with Ian Taggart, and the man was so damn in love with his wife. Hell, it would be sickening if it wasn't so, well, appealing. And cute. Yeah, it was actually fucking cute.

And now, as he listened to that tone of adoration in Hunter's voice, Riley couldn't help but wonder what it would be like to have a woman waiting for him at home. Someone who worried about where he was. Someone who shared hopes and dreams and a life.

The odds of that ever happening were slim to none. Hell, he was edging up against thirty-six, but he'd only ever met one woman who'd truly gotten under his skin. A woman with whom he'd imagined long walks and easy conversations. Along with the more standard fantasies involving heated passion and sweaty, naked nights, of course.

Natasha Black.

Her tall, slim body with her just-perfect breasts. The cool gray eyes that could cut like a knife, and that wide, gorgeous mouth that was made for naughty things. Just the thought of her made his cock stiffen and his fingers crave the smooth brush of her skin. She, however, had very soundly shut him down without so much as a movie and popcorn between them.

Just one more reason not to come back to Los Angeles, because why intentionally rub his nose in something he couldn't have? And yet here he was again.

Not, however, for much longer. This was supposed to be his vacation, after all, and after his last operation with McKay-Taggart, he damn well deserved it. Especially since the operation had been in Los Angeles's backyard. Fucking Taggart. Riley had told Big Tag that he didn't do LA, and Big Tag had just shot him that cocky *I'm in charge here* grin, then informed Riley that Malibu and LA were two completely different cities. When Riley had retorted that they were both in the same damn county, Big Tag had told him to pull up his flowered pink panties and get with the fucking program.

So Riley had hauled his manly brief-covered ass to Malibu and the mission. What the fuck, right? At least the assignment hadn't been in the damn city limits. But he'd been all too happy to leave Malibu-that-wasn't-LA after the mission.

As for today, the layover was a necessary evil, and Riley had never intended to leave the airport.

But now here he was again, right smack dab in the middle of Los Angeles, getting his ass kicked as usual.

Apparently, he never learned.

As soon as two of Hunter's men arrived to take custody of Froggy, Riley and Hunter took the back stairs down to the parking lot. "How badly did I screw with your schedule?" Hunter asked as he leaned against a midnight blue Range Rover.

"No worries," Riley assured him, even though the truth was that he was itching to get the hell out of there. His flight had arrived just after noon, and his connection to vacation-land wasn't scheduled until after midnight. He'd texted Hunter from the tarmac to see if his friend wanted to pop over to LAX for a post-lunch libation, but instead Hunter had begged a favor.

Apparently, Froggy had been in Hunter's sights for a while, but the little worm was familiar with the members of the Stark International security team and getting close was proving tricky. Hunter was about to call in outside help when Riley had phoned, and Hunter had recruited his friend to play the point man.

Which meant that instead of getting a drinking companion, he'd gotten a punch in the face.

"I'd give you a ride back and shoot the shit," Hunter said, "but thanks to your good work, my dance card is full. I'll have one of my guys give you a lift, though."

"Fair enough," Riley said, then promised to send his friend a postcard from China.

"Why China?" Hunter asked as a tall blond man in jeans, a black T-shirt, and a shoulder harness headed toward them.

"Why not?" Riley shot back, making Hunter laugh.

Moments later, he was in the passenger seat of the blond man's tricked-out Grand Cherokee, they were heading South on the 405 toward LAX, and Riley was pondering the question. Why *had* he picked China? His first instinct had been Hawaii. He'd imagined himself watching girls in bikinis as he kicked back on the beach with a thriller in one hand and a beer in the other. But somehow, Hawaii didn't seem far enough away. He wanted to get lost. To go someplace completely unfamiliar. Where he couldn't even read the signs. Some place that forced him to think.

And then, maybe, he'd think about what the fuck he wanted to do next. Because the truth was, he'd been at loose ends for one hell of a long time. But damned if he knew how to tie those ends up.

"Mind if I play some tunes?" his companion asked.

"Go ahead. Sorry I'm bad company. I'm already sliding into vacation mode."

The guy chuckled. "No worries," he said, then pushed a button on the console and filled the interior with ghetto rap as his blond head and shoulders gyrated to the music. Riley dropped his head back, letting the music pound against his brain.

They were almost to the airport when he miraculously felt the buzz of his phone in his pocket despite the deep thrum of the music. He fished it out, checked the Caller ID, then grinned as he gestured toward the volume. "Sorry, man. Do you mind?"

The guy waved off the question with a good-natured shrug, then flicked the radio off right as Riley took the call. "Hey man, how's London? I'm about to get the hell out of your neck of the woods."

"You dick," Lyle Tarpin said. "You're in town and you don't even call?"

"Hello? Because you're in fucking London. You're there doing publicity bullshit. Or am I wrong?" One of Riley's oldest friends, Lyle Tarpin was fast rocketing into one of Hollywood's most bankable stars. He was also Natasha's boss, and when Riley had been in town about a year ago consulting on one of Lyle's movies, she'd once again firmly shut down Riley's advances. At which point Riley resolved to quit trying. He was a lot of things, but not a masochist, and going after Natasha Black was like beating his head against a very hard—but very pretty—brick wall.

"Shipping out bright and early tomorrow."

"Ah, hell. I'm sorry I missed you."

"Me, too."

There was a pause, and Riley was about to ask about Lyle's wife, Laine, when Lyle jumped back in with, "Listen, I need a favor."

"Anything, man. You know that."

"Can you recommend a security company? I need to hire a bodyguard."

Riley understood that. He'd been in town when Lyle had met his wife, Laine, and had seen the boy fall hard and fast. No way would he leave without making sure she was well protected. Whether Laine wanted to be or not.

"Have you talked with Hunter?"

"Ryan Hunter? Not about this, and I won't. He's got his hands full with something, and I don't want him to feel obligated to cover for a friend."

Riley scowled, thinking of his early conversation with Hunter. "What's he chasing?"

"Who knows? But I figure a man like Damien Stark gets a lot of threats. And you know damn well that Ryan's going to take each and every one of them seriously."

It was a good point. Suddenly Hunter's cushy job for the billionaire seemed a little less cushy.

"I have a few names I could give you. Does Laine have any personality preferences for her security detail?" Most of the celebrity wives he'd dealt with preferred a bodyguard to fade into the background like wallpaper. But Sugar Laine was not most celebrity wives. She had a sweetness and charm about her that set her apart from the crowd.

Lyle's brow furrowed in confusion. "Sugar?" he asked. Lyle was the only one who called Sugar by her given name. Everyone else called her by her surname, Laine. "Oh, no. She's going with me on the tour."

"Oh." Honestly, Riley should have assumed as much. "Then who are you protecting?"

"Natasha," Lyle said, the name sinking like a stone in Riley's stomach. "A couple of things have happened, and I just want to play it safe."

Things?

Riley didn't bother to ask for details. If Lyle was worried, then so was he. Without even being aware he'd made a decision, he snapped his fingers for the driver's attention, then pointed toward the next exit. As the car veered across three lanes of traffic, Riley clutched the door handle. Not for safety, but because otherwise he'd have put his fist through the glass out of worry for Tasha. "Are you at your office? I'm on my way."

"What? Why—"

"I'm staying," Riley said in the kind of voice that brooked no argument. "I'll watch out for Natasha."

Chapter Two

"You're sure you don't mind?" Allison McCray asks. *Allison McCray Kealing*, I remind myself, though it's still hard to get used to. Aly is my oldest friend, and she and I bonded over twenty-five years ago in nursery school, both at the tender age of three.

"Sweetie, you're pregnant and your husband's out of town. I'll bring you whatever you want." I reach up to adjust the earpiece that is perpetually attached to my head while I'm at work. "Just give me the list."

"You're a doll. I'm not technically on bedrest, but the doctor told me I should stay in bed as much as possible these last three weeks. And of course Ben translates that into a carved-in-stone edict. You know how he is."

The truth is, I *don't* know how he is. Not really. An attorney, Allison had temporarily moved from Los Angeles to Manhattan two years ago because of some huge corporate case that was eating her life. The case finally settled, and when she came back, she was not only married, but two months pregnant.

Which means that I've only known Ben for the last six months, and during that time my boss's exploding career has been keeping me crazy busy. All I know is that he works on the business side of one of the networks, that he dotes on Aly, and that she's convinced he hung the moon. For the time being, that's good enough for me.

"Got it," I say, after scribbling down the list she rattles off to me, although it's so short I don't know why I bothered. "No ice cream? No pickles?"

"Don't tease the pregnant woman," she warns. "It's like poking a bear. And you might as well throw in some of those fudge brownie bites. The ones in the bakery section."

Considering every item on her list is from the bakery section, the cookie aisle, or the frozen dessert section, I'm thinking that Little Bit is going to share her momma's sweet tooth.

"Should I grab some Peanut Butter M&Ms at the checkout stand?" I ask.

"Oh, Natasha, this is why we're besties."

I laugh. "Who knew friendship could be bought with chocolate?"

"Ha! And seriously, thanks. Just let yourself in when you get here. I'm in the bedroom with my headphones on watching my way through the entire Marvel catalog. Just don't tell my boss. I'm supposed to be reviewing depositions since I'm not technically on maternity leave yet."

"Your secret's safe with me." I check the time and do a quick calculation. "I've probably got another three hours of work here. Lyle's heading to London tomorrow to start the publicity tour for *M. Sterious*, and I'm buried in checklists."

"Tell him congratulations. I'm all caught up with the Blue Zenith films. I can't wait to see him as *M. Sterious*. The trailer looks amazing."

"The movie's even better," I say before we end the call. Then I drop my phone on the desk and roll my chair to the bookcase so I can grab one of the rough cut DVDs. I know Lyle won't mind if I give my friend an advance peek, but just to be safe, I lever myself out of the chair, grab my portfolio, and cross the open area to the closed door of his private office.

The condo was originally Lyle's residence, but he converted it to an office when he moved to Venice Beach. Now the entire living room/kitchen combination is my domain, and since we're on the thirtieth floor, my desk has a stunning view all the way to the Pacific. Can you say job perk?

Even without the stellar view, I'd still love this office. Not only is the interior roomy and inviting, but as part of a high-end development in Century City, the building has great security. And that's something I've begun to appreciate lately.

A lot.

I shake my head, forcing the thoughts back into the dark little corners of my mind where I store all my unpleasant thoughts and memories. Yes, some creep has clearly taken a liking to me, but LA is a town full of creeps, and as Lyle's assistant, I'm bound to get some of the fallout from his merry band of groupies, right?

Besides, one creepy postcard and an icky email does not a stalker make.

At least that's what I keep telling myself.

I rap on the door to Lyle's private office—formerly his bedroom—then enter when he calls back for me to come in. It's lined with bookshelves now and a large desk fills the space, along with two guest chairs that face the desk and a comfy couch tucked in front of one of the bookshelves.

Usually, it's only Lyle in this room. But it's set up to be a comfortable meeting space, too.

I stand in front of his desk, then hold up the DVD. "Okay if I give this to a friend who's a fan? Normally I wouldn't ask, but she's knocked up and on bedrest, so…"

"Are you kidding? You should know you don't even need to ask."

I do know, but I figure it's a good work policy to never take anything for granted.

"Actually, hand it here," he says, grabbing a Sharpie off his desk. "All pregnant fans on bedrest get autographed DVDs."

I laugh. That's another reason I love my job. Even though Lyle's a total A-lister, he's a great boss, without any of the typical celebrity ego and bullshit that often comes with the Hollywood package.

Not that he doesn't have a dark side—he does, as pretty much the whole world recently discovered when he and Laine got caught up in the kind of scandal that keeps social media hopping. But at his core, he's one hundred percent solid, and one of the best guys I know.

"So what can I help you with?" I ask as he signs the DVD. He gives me back the movie, then scans the desk before glancing up at me with a shrug, obviously realizing there wasn't a thing he needed to do at the office.

My lips twitch. "I told you that you didn't need to come in today. I already sent everything you need to the house yesterday. And," I add with a nod to his computer, "you could have answered all those emails at home."

He frowns, looking slightly abashed, and more than a little charming. It's that combination of farm boy looks and serious sex appeal that helped rocket him to the top.

What I also notice is that he looks a little guilty, too.

"Oh, no, you didn't," I say, dropping into one of the leather chairs opposite his desk. "Please tell me you didn't come all the way to the office just to keep an eye on me."

"You know you can still change your mind and come on the tour."

I slide my portfolio onto his desk before leaning back and crossing my arms. "One, the flight arrangements are already made. Two, half the studio PR department will be there to take care of you. Three, I have big plans for plowing through the insane pile of work I never seem to get to because my boss is so high maintenance."

He rolls his eyes at that. Lyle is so *not* high maintenance.

"Look," I continue, before he can grab control of the conversation, "it's really not a big deal. You're acting like I have some psycho stalker after me, but it was just a creepy postcard and an email." I congratulate myself on sounding convincing. Because yes, I am a bit wigged out. But I also know it's probably nothing. Even so, I'm not going to jog by myself after dark or do a hop-skip routine down an abandoned alley. I'll be smart, and I'll be fine.

And the more I repeat that to myself, the more I believe it.

Bottom line, Lyle is not altering his plans because of me. And I'm not altering mine because some jerk has put me on edge.

"*Just* an email and a postcard? Did you forget that someone tagged the hood of your car?"

I wave that away. There was no reason to believe that was personal. More likely some teens acting out. A conclusion I've told him at least half a dozen times.

"Just do me a favor and stay here. The couch folds out, and it's comfortable."

I roll my eyes. "I have a house in Studio City. Plus a cat I have to feed. I'll be fine."

His phone chimes, indicating that someone is downstairs waiting to be buzzed in. More folks from studio publicity, I assume. "I'll meet them at the door," I say, as he presses the button to authorize them to enter the foyer and operate the elevator.

"We're going to find a compromise," he says as I head out of the room. "I'm not leaving the country unless I'm certain my staff is safe."

I pause long enough to glance over my shoulder at him. "You've read too many action scripts." I see him roll his eyes as I head to the door. "I'm serious," I call out, because I don't want to admit that his concern is making me a little bit nervous. "I'm perfectly safe," I say as I start to open the door. "No one is going to hurt me."

"They damn sure aren't," Riley Blade says as I pull back the door to reveal him leaning against the frame, his arms crossed over his broad chest and his eyes lost behind the kind of dark glasses that hide a man's secrets. "Not on my watch."

He smiles, wide and slow, then tugs the glasses down with the tip of his finger to reveal gold-flecked brown eyes that he uses to rake his gaze down my body and then back up again, leaving my skin unexpectedly—and unwillingly—humming.

"Don't worry, Tasha," he says when his eyes meet mine. "I promise I'll keep you safe."

Chapter Three

Within seconds, Riley has stepped over the threshold, and Lyle has emerged from his office.

As for me, I've been standing like an idiot, my feet practically glued to the floor as my mind whirs through the situation, finally arriving at one painful, unpleasant, inescapable conclusion—my boss sold me out.

Son of a *bitch*.

Furious, I whirl toward Lyle, only to find myself that much closer to Riley, which really wasn't my intent. The man exudes a sensual kind of heat that's hard to ignore—and believe me, I'm trying. I neither want nor need Riley Blade in my life, and I really don't understand what the hell he's doing here and why he's talking like he already knows my situation.

Except, of course, I *do* know, which takes me straight back to that whole *my boss sold me out* analysis.

"Seriously?" I snap at Lyle, who holds his hands up in self-defense as he starts to talk, presumably intending to calm me down.

"Now, just a second, Tasha," Riley says, but that's as far as he gets because I round on him, my throat full of tears and my eyes burning from the strain of not letting them escape.

"Do *not* call me that. Dammit, Riley, you of all people should know not to call me that."

I turn away, because if I look at him I know I'll burst into tears, and as I do, I see Lyle's baffled expression.

Oddly, that gives me comfort. It means that Riley Blade kept my secret. I'd never really doubted that he would. I've known Riley since I was twenty-two, and even though I've made it perfectly clear that I'm not interested in dating him, that doesn't mean that I don't trust him.

But even so, it's nice to know I was right.

"Okay, hold up," Lyle says. "What do you mean, Riley *of all people*? You two barely spoke twelve words to each other the entire time Riley was consulting." What he doesn't add is that those twelve words mostly consisted of me saying no to his repeated advances.

I look between the two men, both of whom I respect, and feel my shoulders go slack as the fight drains out of me. "Dammit, Lyle. Why'd you pull Blade into this?"

"He didn't," Riley says gently. "He called to ask me to recommend a bodyguard. That's all."

I scowl at him. "Then recommend somebody, dammit."

"Come on, Natasha," he says. "You know what an arrogant son-of-a-bitch I am. Do you really think there's someone in this town I trust more than me?"

The answer, of course, is no.

I run a finger through my hair, tucking one long strand behind my ear in frustration.

"Let's sit," Lyle says. "We'll bring Riley up to speed, and then we'll figure out what to do next. And if you want to take pity on me, you can explain to me why you two know each other a hell of a lot better than I thought you did."

"My dad and Riley were part of the same FBI SWAT team," I explain grudgingly once we're settled. I'm on one section of the L-shaped sofa, and I slip my feet out of my heels and tuck them up under me, then pull a pillow into my lap, as if somehow that will keep me safe. Then I draw a breath and look down, my focus on the geometric pattern of the area rug. "I don't—The memories," I say, switching gears. "It's not a time I like to think about."

I glance up to see Lyle nod from where he sits in an Eames chair, his back against the buttery leather. He never knew my father, but I told Lyle about my dad one long night when he was shooting *The Price of Ransom*, a true crime movie about a horrific kidnapping. Since my father had been killed in the line of duty during a nightmarish raid in a human trafficking case, I'd been more than a little edgy during filming, and I'd shared more than I usually did with my boss. Lyle had been kind. He'd thanked me for sharing, told me that I'd helped him center the character, and then offered his condolences for my loss.

That night, honestly, had been a turning point for me. Before, I'd liked my job. After that day, I knew my boss would have my loyalty forever.

Now, Lyle looks over at Riley, who's sharing the sofa with me, albeit on the other section. His long, muscled legs are stretched out in front of him, and he's leaning back, as if he's completely at home. It's not until Lyle speaks that I remember just how well he and Riley know each other. "Didn't you leave the FBI for the private sector after the take-down of a human trafficking ring in East LA went south?" Lyle asks.

Riley nods.

To his credit, Lyle doesn't look at me. But he's a smart man; he knows there's history between me and Riley—and more than the basic fact that Riley and my father worked together. Lyle doesn't know the details, though. And he doesn't ask.

Just one more reason to sing my boss's praises.

As for him expecting Blade to babysit me...

I shift on the sofa, my head tilted so that my eyes are fixed on Riley. "I don't need you to stay."

"No?"

"No," I assure him, then turn to Lyle. "Really. No."

Riley sits up and leans forward, his elbows on his knees. "Dammit, Natasha, you know I'm good at what I do—and with all the work I've been doing with McKay-Taggart, I'm even better at the bodyguard gig than I was before. I can keep you safe. Don't be an idiot and turn down my offer."

He aims those dark eyes at me, and I swallow. With that piercing gaze and his sexy swath of five-o'clock shadow over a strong, rugged jaw, the man really does ooze sensuality. More than that, though, he gives the impression of strength. Of solidity.

Of safety, pure and simple.

And, yeah, some part of me wants to know that he has my back.

I'm going to cave—I know it. I'm not stupid, and now that I've seen Riley again, up close and personal, I don't want Lyle to give in and hire me a rent-a-cop.

I want Riley. I just don't *want* Riley.

But I'm damn sure not going to admit it just yet. Do that, and I'll never manage to erase his smug expression.

He says he wants the job? Fine. He can work to convince me. At least then we'll be on somewhat even footing.

Not that I've ever felt like I'm on even ground around Riley. I'm far too attracted to the man, and always have been.

I'll let Riley watch over me. But that's as far as things will go between us. I'll tell him the same thing I told him when he consulted with Lyle. No passes. No flirting. Business only, or else I'll shut it down and find my own damn bodyguard.

I don't say a word, but he must have picked up on my acquiescence, because he looks between Lyle and me and then says, "So fill me in, and we can talk about the best approach."

I meet Lyle's eyes, and when my cheeks start to heat with a rising blush, I nod, silently urging him to tell the story.

"Matthew Holt's pushing me hard to sign on to a new project. A thriller with an erotic edge."

"Nice," Riley says, his eyes cutting to me. I'm sure the look is simply a question mark—*What does this have to do with Natasha?* But to me it feels personal, as if he's sizing up my own erotic potential.

I know that's ridiculous—more than that, I know that my reaction is fueled by the simple fact that I know where this story is heading—but I can't deny the sudden sense of awareness that floods my body, pooling most intensely at my breasts and between my thighs.

I force my attention back to Lyle and keep it locked there.

"The thing is, I really want to do the project—Holt's company, Hardline Entertainment, is doing some terrific work—but the script's not finished, so I'm hesitant to commit. But the screenwriter is willing to shoot me pages as she works for feedback, which is great. But if I'm going to be able to comment intelligently, I need to have a better sense of the world."

"The world?"

"Most of the story takes place in a BDSM club."

"Wait a sec. Any chance this movie is based on a book?"

Lyle's eyes widen; he's clearly as surprised as I am.

"Yeah," Lyle says. "*Her Secret Service.*"

Riley laces his fingers behind his head and leans back. "That's fucking awesome. Are you playing Zan?"

"What the hell? How did you know that?"

"Serena Dean-Miles," Riley says. "She's the author, right? It's not common knowledge, but she bases most of her books on real McKay-Taggart missions. Too bad you're not starring in a book featuring me. I'm way cooler than Zan. Of course, she hasn't written that book yet." He buffs his nails on his chest. "I guess she's saving the best for last."

"Talk about a coincidence," Lyle says, glancing at me. I force a smile past the unpleasant taste of jealousy that has coated my mouth. I try to swallow it down. After all, I don't even know if Serena Dean-Miles is single, much less if she's involved with Riley. But he does know her... And she does write incredibly sexy books...

Stop it.

I have no reason to be jealous. Primarily because there is nothing—*nothing*—between Riley and me.

"At any rate, I wanted to visit a club," Lyle says, shifting the conversation back on track and saving me from my runaway thoughts.

"Ah, the plot thickens." Riley once again focuses on me. I keep my eyes on Lyle. But I feel the heat rise in my cheeks.

"Apparently Matthew has a membership at a local club, so we went."

I risk a glance toward Riley, who doesn't look the least bit shocked. "Did he take you to The Reef? The club in Malibu?"

Lyle tilts his head, and it's his turn to be impressed. "Didn't realize you had such intimate knowledge of the local club scene. But no, it wasn't The Reef. We went to The Firehouse. The LA branch of an exclusive Chicago club, actually. Matthew's a member."

"Since Natasha's in the thick of this, I'm assuming she's included in the *we*?"

"She is." Lyle pauses to look my direction, as if to see if I want to chime in. I don't. At the moment, I'm happy to stay mute. It gives me the chance to remember all I saw inside The Firehouse...and to wonder exactly how well Riley knows what goes on in a place like that.

"I took Sugar, of course. But honestly, I wanted Nat along, too, especially since I intend for her to sit in on the meetings with the writer. Plus, she has a good eye and a good memory. So she went as Matthew's date."

"Go on," Riley said, at which point Lyle shrugged.

"That's pretty much it. We went, and the Dom in Residence gave us a brief tour. It's a club that's conceived in three parts. You enter into a pretty typical bar, although none of the drinks are alcoholic, and it has a much more sexual decor and a significantly more sensual vibe. A lot of leather and some submissives and slaves at their owners' feet, but for the most part the first room is cocktail tables and chit-chat. The main area is open, broken up into different sections for different scenes with a variety of equipment. I suppose you'd call that the dungeon. Beyond that are smaller, more private rooms. The doors can be locked or left open if you don't mind—or want—an audience."

"I'm guessing you stayed primarily in the dungeon."

Lyle nods. "Primarily. But there were several open doors in the back, and Matthew took us through quite a few."

"I see." Riley turns to look straight at me, those mahogany-brown eyes silently demanding that I tell him the rest.

And, damn me, I hustle to obey. "That's pretty much it. We didn't get involved in any scenes. We went in on Matthew's membership, and we stayed in that main section. It was—interesting."

I'm not about to admit how fascinated I'd been by the vibrant sensuality that had surrounded me, including full-on sexual gratification—mixed with more than a little sexual punishment.

I'd been shocked at first—and then a bit turned on. A fact I'd confessed to no one, and fully intended to keep to myself until the end of time. But secret or not, it was true, and my sex ached right now from nothing more than the memory of it.

"So you didn't participate, but you were visible?"

I nod.

"And then?"

"And then we left." I swallow. "And the next morning I found the postcard underneath the windshield wiper of my car."

"Postcard," he repeats. "What did it say?"

I lick my lips, then recite, "*Whore. You're mine now.*" As I speak, Lyle passes Riley his phone where, I know, he keeps a picture of the postcard.

Riley glances at it, his brow furrowed and his mouth curved down into a frown. "Pencil?"

Lyle shakes his head. "I had a friend in the police department take a look. Detective Garrison. Dean Garrison."

"I've worked with him," Riley says. "Good man."

Lyle nods, but continues about the postcard. "According to Garrison, someone traced the words onto the postcard using carbon paper."

Riley nods slowly. "And the image of lips on the other side. *Rocky Horror* lips. Which might or might not be relevant. No fingerprints?" he asks me.

"No," I say. "We didn't check right away—I thought it was creepy but not scary at first. Just someone jerking my chain, you know? I didn't even put it together with The Firehouse, honestly. Not until the email came. That's when Lyle had Garrison come by. And he took it to the lab so they could dust for prints. Not a one. Well, except for mine."

"Where's the email?"

"Next photo," Lyle says, and Riley uses his thumb to scroll through. I don't need to walk to him to know what he's seeing. The image is burned into my mind. A woman on her knees, a collar around her neck, her hands bound behind her and a ball gag in her mouth. Beneath the image, in a handwriting-style font, the message announces, *This is how you should be. Bitch, bitch, you're mine, little bitch.*

Remembering, I hug myself.

"I can see why you'd be disturbed," Riley says, and I exhale in relief, only then realizing that I'd been afraid he was going to say the very thing I keep repeating to Lyle. That it's nothing. Just bullshit. No big deal.

Except that isn't true, and I know it. And, weirdly, the fact that Riley is validating that horrible reality makes me feel better.

"The email address?"

"Bogus," Lyle says. "I have a friend in Austin who's a whiz at that kind of thing. Noah said it was set up on a computer at a library in Northridge. After that, nothing."

"Okay. Anything else?" Riley asks, and I shake my head. "Nothing?" he presses. "No sensations of being followed? No familiar faces around corners? Unusual calls or hang ups?"

"Nothing," I assure him.

"Except the paint," Lyle mentions.

"Paint?"

I shrug. "Someone tagged my car. But I was running some errands in a dicey section of the Valley. It was probably just teenagers. I mean, surely whoever sent the postcard and email didn't follow me halfway across the San Fernando Valley just to spray-paint the word *cunt* on my car."

"Probably not," Riley says. "Or maybe that was a test run. Maybe your stalker was testing his own limits. He got close to your car last time. Next time he'll try to get close to you."

I shiver, then hug myself. Riley notices and comes to sit down next to me, his weight shifting the cushion so that I end up closer to him than is comfortable. Then he puts his hand on my thigh, the sensation warm and safe and more than a little distracting.

I scoot over, tugging my leg out from under his touch. He hesitates, then stands. And, dammit all, I not only feel like a raging bitch, but I desperately miss the comfort of that touch.

Lyle, thankfully, fills the awkward gap. "It has to be someone from the club. The timing. The image of the ball-gag. That's the only explanation."

"I'm not sure it's the only," Riley counters. "But it's the most likely."

"So you're saying that some guy at the club saw me, became obsessed with me, and decided to stalk me?" The idea seems both utterly absurd and dead-on point.

"Pretty much," Riley acknowledges.

"So how do we find him? Set up hidden cameras and wait for him to put another note under my wiper?"

"He won't go that route again. Not now that you might be paying attention."

"Then what? I just wait?"

"That's one plan," Riley says. "I think the better one is to draw him out."

I hug the pillow closer. "How do I do that?"

"You don't. *We* do."

My instinct is to argue, but I tamp it back. Riley and I both know that I'm not tackling this on my own. "Okay, we. How do *we* draw him out?"

"Simple," he says. "Tomorrow night, I'm going to take you to The Firehouse."

Chapter Four

"I can't believe you're going to a BDSM club," Aly says as she digs into the breakfast tacos I've brought with me. "I'm so jealous." She falls back against her pillows with a sigh. "Then again, I'm so tired of being in bed that I'd be jealous if you told me you were going to Starbucks."

"I wouldn't need to borrow an outfit if I was going to Starbucks," I point out as I step into her roomy closet. I pull out a pair of buttery soft, black leather pants along with a matching leather overbust corset with a front zipper and side laces to adjust the fit and the amount of cinch.

I carry them both out of the closet and hold up the two hangers, one in each hand. "And why exactly do you have clothes that are stamped with the BDSM seal of approval?"

"Oh, please. That's totally tame. And it's from my days clubbing in Manhattan. You might as well keep both of them." She points to her belly. "After this little guy makes his appearance, I doubt I'll fit back into them. And my boobs were always too big for that thing, anyway."

I laugh. "Thanks a lot for the cold, hard truth." I've got a slim build, and the barely-a-B-cup tits that go along with that.

All she says is, "Trust me," which seems like a total non sequitur. "Go on," she continues, with a regal wave of her hand. "Try it all on."

I shrug, then strip down to my panties and step into the pants. Since I've known Aly forever, there's not a bit of modesty between us, but the truth is, I've never been the shy type. Probably fortunate, I think, since I'm heading to a BDSM club tonight.

"How come you don't already have something to wear?" Aly asks. "Didn't you go with Lyle and his wife and that producer recently?"

"Yeah, but I pretty much blew the dress code that day, I think."

Maybe not, because Matthew obviously knew the drill, and he said I looked fine. But he also knew that we were there only to observe, so no one really cared if my plain black leggings and simple silk tank were completely wrong for the occasion and location. In other words, I'd worn an outfit that telegraphed that I was there to observe, not to play.

According to Riley, this time I'm not going to observe, I'm going to get noticed. The goal is to draw the stalker out so that Riley can swoop in. According to him, we're going to slide into the rhythm of the club. Make ourselves noticed by whoever. Lure them out. I'm not entirely sure how he intends to do that. But I'm definitely the bait. And the bait requires a wardrobe.

I tug up the back zipper and allow myself a happy sigh. The pants are a perfect fit, soft and pliable, and they hug me like a second skin.

"Damn," Aly says. "I guess it's just as well I'm giving them to you. You look so much better than I ever did. No—" she says, before I can protest. "It's an empirical fact. You have an ass, and my butt is as flat as a pancake. You, my friend, own those pants. All I could manage was to wear them."

I don't say it out loud, but I have to admit she's right. Not about how Aly looked in them—I never saw her—but about the fact that they look damn good on me. More than that, I genuinely like them. The weight of the leather. The tactile sensation of the material against my skin. I feel sexy and powerful, and as far as I'm concerned, that's a good thing. Because I started this day feeling confused and out of sorts.

And not entirely because of my stalker.

With a frown, I push thoughts of Riley from my head. I'd spent the night tossing and turning as he'd invaded my Firehouse-filled dreams, inserting himself into the situations and scenes I'd witnessed during the research tour of the place. I'd awakened just seconds before a massive orgasm ripped over me, my skin hot, my nipples tight, and my inner thighs slick with desire.

It wasn't the first time Riley had invaded my fantasies over the years, but it had definitely been the most intense, and the most frustrating. And not just because I know damn well that nothing is going to develop between us outside of my dreams, but also because I woke without any memory of what he'd done to get me in such a state.

So, yeah, I felt a little cheated.

"Quit admiring your excellent ass and put on the top," Aly says.

"What?" Her words startle me out of my thoughts and I realize that I'm still wearing my *M. Sterious* cast and crew tank top. "Oh, sorry." I tug it over my head, then unlatch the front hook of my bra and let it fall behind me.

"Now I feel better about my ass," Aly says. "At least I have tits."

"Hey, I brought you breakfast tacos. You're not allowed to be mean to me."

"Just soothing my bruised ego," she says. "You look hot." She broke off to look me over from head to toe. "Well, half-naked and hot. And I look like a beached whale."

"You look amazing," I say sincerely as I grab the corset and connect the two halves of the zipper. "You're glowing."

She rolls her eyes, but I can see she looks pleased. "That's what Ben always says, but I figured he was just blowing smoke up my ass."

"Totally true," I tell her, then glance down at my chest. "This can't be right." The leather just sort of hangs on me, not nearly as flattering as I'd hoped.

With a laugh, Aly motions me over, then reaches for the laces at the side. She tugs and tightens, then repeats the process on the other side, binding me into the thing. "Now look," she says.

I turn, do as she says, then gasp.

I've got tits. I mean, I've got actual, bouncy, overflowing tits.

"I think I love you," I tell Aly. "And I know I love this corset."

She laughs. "Told you so. And you know who's really going to love it? Riley."

A tingle of anticipation spreads though me, but I tamp it down. I don't need to be thinking about Riley that way. "Just so long as I blend at the club. No," I correct. "No blending. The idea is to be seen."

Aly bites her lower lip as she studies me.

"What?" I demand.

"It's just—" She makes a face, then barrels on. "Are you sure you're okay doing this?"

My eyes go wide. "If it gets a stalker out of my life? Yeah, I think I can deal with going to a club."

"No, I don't mean the club," she corrects. "I mean Riley. Maybe you outgrew it—maybe you're just ignoring it—but I still remember."

I lick my lips, my mouth suddenly dry. "Remember what?"

She rolls her eyes. "You. Riley. All of it. You used to have the biggest crush on him, and don't even try to deny it, because I'm the one you happy danced in front of when he finally noticed you. I mean, you two could have been a thing if it weren't for—"

"Stop," I say. "None of that matters anymore."

"Why?" I can hear the sympathy in her voice, and I hate it. "Because of your dad? Come on, Nat. You can't really—"

"Just drop it," I snap, my voice thick. I turn away, not wanting my best friend in the whole world to see the way I'm keeping my eyes unnaturally wide in an attempt to keep a fresh wave of tears at bay.

I draw in a breath, then turn to her. "I'm sorry for snapping," I say, meaning it. Where Riley and my dad and that whole horrible year are concerned, my nerves are always frayed. "But I'm thirty years old now. I'm beyond crushes." I've moved on to safe. To practical.

"I don't think you're ever beyond crushes," Aly says gently. "And I'm going back to my original question—are you sure you're going to be okay? Because when you open your door tonight and Riley sees you... Well, sweetie, I'll bet you a million dollars that boy's cock is going to bust right out of his jeans."

"You don't have a million dollars," I point out, fighting a smile.

She lifts a shoulder in a casual shrug. "Won't need it. Because this is one bet I'm totally going to win."

* * * *

I'm still thinking of Aly's ridiculous bet later that evening as I feel the leather mold to my ass when I bend to scratch Pumpkin behind the ears. A ginger-colored mutt of a cat, I'd found her hiding behind a dumpster when I'd gone to look for packing boxes before moving into my current Studio City rental. She's now the most pampered indoor cat in Southern California, and at the moment, she's annoyed with me for not picking her up to cuddle.

"I'm sorry, baby." She's a kneader, and I don't want to risk her claws in the pristine leather—or on my bare shoulder, for that matter. "Come on. I'll open a can of tuna."

I see her ears twitch—I know she can understand me—but she's in a pissy enough mood that she doesn't follow me to the kitchen. Not, that is, until I start to run the can opener. Then the lure of tuna overcomes her annoyance and she trots into the kitchen, does a figure-eight between my legs, then parks herself by her Miss Kitty placemat that I keep by the sliding glass door that leads into the backyard.

I hear her purr as I put the plate down and know that all is forgiven.

Too bad all problems can't be solved as easily.

Since I'm in the kitchen anyway, I open the fridge and pull out an already open bottle of Chardonnay. I tell myself I only want a drink because it's late summer and the house is warm and I'm decked out in meteorologically inappropriate leather.

Which is ridiculous.

I want a drink because I'm going to a BDSM club.

Or, more accurately, because I'm going to a BDSM club with Riley.

I fill the glass, toss back a long swallow, and for about the millionth time wonder what the hell I was thinking.

That's not a question I have time to consider, however, because the doorbell rings and my stomach pretty much drops to the floor.

That boy's cock is going to bust right out of his jeans.

Aly's words once again ring like klaxons in my head, and as I hurry to the front door, I can't erase the image of faded blue denim riding low on Riley's hips, the material hugging his thighs, and his equipment so hard that the button fly is about to burst. *Oh, dear Lord in heaven.*

By the time I reach the door my mouth is dry and I've decided to murder my best friend.

As soon as my hand reaches the doorknob, I hesitate, remembering not only the situation, but the town I live in. "Who is it?"

I don't have a peephole, something I've been bugging my landlord about since I moved in. And while there used to be windows on either side of the door, the glass was replaced with frosted glass bricks several owners ago, allowing light in but no prying eyes. Unfortunately, the privacy means no looking out, either.

"It's me. Riley."

I flip the deadbolt, unfasten the chain, and tug open the door.

Then I freeze. I absolutely, freaking freeze.

He's standing in front of me in tight leather pants that hug every curve, enticingly revealing just how well-endowed the man truly is. I drag my gaze up, and the last bit of moisture in my mouth dries up like the Sahara. He's wearing a matching black vest, but is shirtless underneath.

Honestly, I'm not sure how he's finding the time to help me, because he is so incredibly ripped that he must live at a gym. Not only does he have the most perfect six-pack I've ever had the pleasure of seeing, but there are two enticing cuts of muscle at his hips angling down like twin arrows beneath his pants, as if pointing the way to heaven.

Beads of sweat form at the back of my neck, and I'm thinking that my decision to wear only a tiny thong under my own leather was a mistake. Because, Oh. My. God.

I force my gaze the rest of the way up until my eyes reach his, and I see amusement dancing in the specks of gold.

"Hey, beautiful," he says, the deep tones of his voice doing a number on my insides. "Are you ready?"

Chapter Five

Riley considered it a miracle that he didn't blow his wad right then.

Over the years, he'd seen Natasha Black in everything from a bikini at a community picnic to a sequined gown at a charity ball. But this...

Christ almighty, his cock was as hard as steel and his balls were so tight that he had to call on all his strength not to pull her to him, kiss her senseless, then fuck her hard over the back of the living room couch, which had the advantage of being the nearest piece of furniture he could see.

Had he really asked her if she was ready?

Ready?

He'd lost all perspective as to what that word meant because he'd never been more ready in his life.

He saw her swallow, then look up into his eyes. The heat he saw reflected there shot straight to his already painfully hard cock, but it was the fear and uncertainty that made him step cautiously over the threshold.

"Natasha?" he pressed, realizing she hadn't answered his question. "Are you okay?"

She nodded, then licked her lips, the sight of that pretty pink tongue sending his mind spinning off into fantasies of her kneeling in front of him in nothing but a thong and that seriously hot bustier as he fisted her hair and fucked her mouth hard and fast, those perfect lips stroking his shaft as he thrust deeper and deeper until he finally exploded, and she sucked and swallowed every last drop.

He reached out for the doorjamb, steadying himself against the fast and furious intensity of that unexpected image.

Drawing in a deep breath, he forced himself to focus. He wouldn't go so far as to call himself a Dom, though where sex was concerned, he couldn't deny that he was all about control. Still, he'd been in more than his share of clubs and had been undercover as a Dom on more than one occasion. He knew how to give pleasure, and he knew how to use pain, and he got off on manipulating both. Most of all, he knew how to subjugate his own needs to that of his sub, and how to push her just to the edge of her comfort zone, but never over.

Right now, Natasha was very clearly at the edge of her comfort zone. And Riley needed to tell his own damn libido to chill the fuck out. This wasn't about the two of them; this had nothing to do with the way he craved her. Hell, he didn't even know if she would find pleasure in submitting. Damn, though, he wanted to find out. Just the thought made him weak with desire.

But he had to shut that down. This wasn't about his need for control or her submission. On the contrary, this trip to The Firehouse was an act—hell, it was an elaborate scene—and he needed to make sure that she understood the rules and that they both understood the boundaries.

He stepped over the threshold, and she immediately moved back, giving him room to enter.

"You're nervous."

It wasn't a question, and she didn't respond.

He hooked a finger under her chin and tilted her head up so she was forced to look at him. "It's okay," he said. "I've got you."

A tiny smile danced on her lips. "You're what makes me the most nervous."

Her words were barely a whisper, and he had to concentrate to hear them. But hear them he did, and though he wished those words gave him hope, all they did was fill him with regret.

He drew a breath, then released it slowly. "What I'm about to say should be part of a longer conversation. There should be back and forth and discussion. There should be conversation and revelation. But we don't have time for that. The Firehouse works on reservations, and if we miss ours, we don't go tonight. So I'm just going to say this, and you think about it, and we'll talk later, okay?"

Because he knew Tasha, he expected an argument. So he was pretty damn surprised when all she did was nod.

"I get that I make you nervous," he said, "especially since we're about to walk into a sex club. More than that, I know why. And it's not because I want you—although you know damn well that I do. Hell, I remember the first time I saw you as a woman, and not just as Eddie's daughter. And it wasn't when you wore those short skirts or flirted with the other guys—and don't think I didn't know you were interested in me—it was when you had your guard down. When you'd come to the hospital after a mission to wait with us for news when someone had been hurt. Or when you'd bring bagels during an all-night briefing, then fall asleep in the reception area with an open paperback beside you because you wanted to see your dad one more time before he went into the field."

He saw the tears well in her eyes, but he didn't even pause.

"I asked you out the morning of that raid—and, yeah, I know you remember it. And we were both a wreck after your father died. You turned me down three days later. You came to my apartment, told me not to say a word, and then said that you didn't think we should ever try to see each other. That it hurt too much."

A tear snaked down her cheek. "Riley—"

"No." The word was hard. A command. "Let me finish."

"Do you know why I call you Tasha?" he asked, then continued before she could answer. "It's not because he did. Or not exactly. It's because you remind me of him. Loyal and strong and caring. It's because I admire you, and I always have. I always will." He drew in a breath. "But I also understand you, and I respect you. I've stayed away. I haven't pushed—not too much, anyway. And when I ended up consulting for Lyle, I never breathed a word to him about our history."

He exhaled, then dragged his fingers through his hair. "The point is that even though we're going to a sex club, I know that whatever show we end up putting on isn't real. I want you, Natasha, make no mistake. But I won't ever push you. Do you understand?"

She nodded, her lips pressed so tight together her mouth was little more than a thin slash of red lipstick.

"Did you know that in the BDSM world, it's always the sub that holds the power?"

Her brow furrowed, and she shook her head.

"It's true. Just like us. Just like now. We're going in because we have to. Because I want you safe, and we're going to figure out who's harassing you. But ultimately all of this is your call, sweetheart. You don't have to do anything you don't want to do."

"And anything that does happen," she began, her voice still soft. "It's all for show? To draw out my stalker?"

"Yes," he said, the word holding the weight of regret, making him truly realize how much he craved reality over fantasy, and driving home just how much this assignment was going to hurt.

And in that moment he knew only one thing for certain. The second this was all wrapped up, he was getting on a plane and getting the hell away from Natasha, his memories, and this goddamn city.

* * * *

Riley used Lyle's car service to take them to The Firehouse. Not only did he not want to deal with parking in downtown Los Angeles, but he also didn't want the road stealing his attention from Natasha. She'd admitted to being nervous because of him, but he was certain it ran much deeper. They were trying to flush out a stalker, after all. She'd be foolish not to be at least a little scared. He got that. And, dammit, he was making it his first priority to make sure she was as comfortable as possible.

"I thought it was interesting that the club's built inside an actual old fire station," she said as the car pulled to a halt in front of the old two-story building tucked in between what now served as low-rent office space on the edge of downtown.

"It makes for a nice big space," Riley said, though he knew she didn't need a reply. She was simply making conversation as she tried to get a handle on her nerves.

"You've never been here before?" she asked, a question to which, once again, she already knew the answer.

"No, you've got the advantage on me," he said with a gentle smile. He took her hand, ridiculously happy when she not only didn't pull away but instead twined her fingers with his. "But I did read up a bit on the place." He'd found some descriptions of the layout and the various levels of membership. And when he'd dug deeper, he'd recognized a few of the owners' names. A few discreet calls later, and he'd learned that Jared Johns was a member. Considering Jared's connections to both the BDSM community and McKay-Taggart, if Riley needed to get any information about the membership at The Firehouse, he knew who to call.

He tilted his head to look at her. "Ready?"

She nodded.

"Lift up your hair."

"Why?"

He only lifted a brow, signaling that even though they might not be inside the club yet, the time to remember their roles had arrived. To his relief, she understood and lifted her long, thick ponytail. Once her neck was exposed, he reached into a satchel he'd left on the floorboards and pulled out a velvet bag. From that, he removed a stunning pounded-silver submissive collar, a single copper ring providing the only hint of color.

Her eyes went wide, and he tensed, mentally readying himself to deflect her protest. Instead, he only heard her slow exhalation of breath.

"That's stunning. Is it…" She trailed off, then licked her lips. "It's a collar, right?"

"It will mark you as mine," he said. "I'm going to put it on you now."

He didn't ask permission, but neither did she protest. On the contrary, she held the ponytail higher and leaned forward as he latched the clasp in the back.

When he leaned back and saw her, a dark goddess with a ring of starfire at her neck, he seriously considered raising the privacy screen to block the driver's view, peeling her out of those pants, and fucking her hard and fast. Just a little appetizer before the main event.

But that, of course, wasn't happening.

Instead, he drew in a breath and reached for the door. "Ready?"

When she didn't answer, he looked back, expecting her to be focused on the façade just beyond their window. But she wasn't. Her attention wasn't on the club, but on him. And when he thought about it, he knew why. She'd seen the inside of the club already. It wasn't a mystery.

But she'd never seen him in that environment. Hell, collaring her had probably only added to her confusion.

"Trust me," he said, the words both gentle and commanding.

He expected her acquiescence—that was the game, after all. What he hadn't expected was the simple truth that colored her voice when she finally spoke.

"I do," she said, the obedience and submission in those two simple words positively slaying him.

That was when he knew the truth. This woman had him by the balls.

More than that, she always had.

Chapter Six

The entrance area to the club is nothing special, but unlike the last time I was here, that reassuring simplicity doesn't calm my nerves. Before, I was nervous about what was behind those doors. Now, I'm nervous about who I'm going through them with.

As Riley instructed, I walk two steps behind him, and though that distance makes me feel alone, when he holds the door open for me and brushes his fingertips over my shoulders as I enter, the shock of connection rushes through me, centering me and reminding me that we're here for a reason, and that there's a point to this game we're playing.

It's a good reminder, actually. Because the more time I spend with Riley the more frustrated with myself I'm becoming. I had my reasons for putting so much distance between us in the past. But now that he's here—even under such odd circumstances—I can't deny that I like it. And more than just the warm and reassuring feeling of knowing he has my back.

The truth is, Aly was right; I've always felt the spark where Riley Blade is concerned. But in the past, I've always been able to extinguish it. To throw water on it and then hurry away before the spark could flicker back into existence.

Yet here I am now, and instead of water, I'm throwing gasoline. And I'm terrified that walking through these doors and into this aptly named club with him will cause the spark to bloom into a full-on blaze.

And what scares me even more is the tiny, secret part of myself that craves the inferno. That longs to burn, as long as it is Riley who reduces me to ashes.

It's an uncomfortable realization, particularly since I've worked so hard to keep my distance from the man. And though I tell myself that this heated craving stems solely from the nature of this situation, I know that isn't true. Riley Blade has always had the power to get under my skin, but I've always had the strength to hold up my walls.

Now, I fear the walls are starting to crumble. And if they do, where will that leave me?

"It'll be okay," Riley says, obviously mistaking my hesitation for trepidation rather than excitement.

"I know," I say, then consider taking the words back when he holds up a leash.

"I want to show you off," he says in response to my raised brows. "More than that, I want to see who takes particular notice of you."

I swallow, but the truth is that the idea of a leash is reassuring. No matter what, I know that Riley will be right there to keep me safe. So I draw a deep breath, then lift my chin as he clamps the leash to the copper loop. He holds one end, and we enter the first area of The Firehouse. Matthew had explained that while there are some even more exclusive clubs that allow drinks, the no alcohol policy at The Firehouse helps ensure that everything that goes on inside these walls is consensual.

That's fine and dandy, but right now I'm really wishing I'd finished off that bottle of Chardonnay.

"There's no guarantee he'll be here tonight," I whisper as we pause at the next set of doors before entering the main play area.

He strokes my cheek, then trails his fingertip over my lips, making me tremble. "Then we'll have to come back," he says, the words firing my senses and my imagination more than I'd like to admit. "Come on, sweetheart. Let's show you off."

He pushes the thick oak door, once again holding it open for me. For a moment, I'm in front of him, and trepidation cuts through me. Then I feel the pressure at my neck and remember the leash. *Riley.*

He's with me even though I can't see him, and the awareness of that constant connection strengthens my resolve.

I take another step and walk all the way into the playroom. I suppose the regulars at the club would call it a dungeon, since there are chains and manacles on the wall and other implements for binding and torture, but it's so clear to me that what is going on here is pleasure and not pain—or, at least not unwanted pain—that I can't think of it as a place meant to subdue and punish.

"You're intrigued," Riley says, and I jump. I hadn't realized he'd come up beside me. "Which scene catches your attention the most?"

I tell myself that I should avoid the question and just let him lead me. Answering would reveal too much. And yet I can't deny that my senses—and my imagination—are on fire.

"There," I say, nodding toward a woman whose arms and legs are strapped to a padded, wooden X. She's naked, and the man standing in front of her is teasing her skin with something that looks almost like an old-fashioned mop, only in leather.

"A flogger," Riley explains when I ask. "And a vibrator," he adds, when I tremble as the man uses what appears to be a Magic Wand on her sex, obviously taking her close to orgasm, but not letting her go all the way.

"Come here," Riley says, taking a seat on a leather bench and forcing me to kneel in front of him, my back to him. He leans forward so that his hands rest on my shoulders and his lips brush my ear, making me shiver. "Tell me what you like about that scene."

"I—I'm not sure."

"No?" His fingers tease my collarbone, and I'm hyperaware of his touch, my skin tingling beneath his fingers. "Is it that she's naked? Does seeing her exposed like that make you hot?"

I swallow. "A little," I admit.

"Can you imagine that's you? Bound and helpless for everyone to see, completely at your master's mercy?" As he speaks, his hand dips lower, caressing the curve of my breast and making my nipples spring to attention. "Is that what turns you on? Is that what you want?"

"No," I whisper. There's something erotic about watching her, about knowing and seeing how aroused she is. But I wouldn't want to be exposed to the world like that. "Not in front of everyone," I say, and only after I've spoken do I realize the full meaning of my words. Because I wouldn't like that in public. But in private…dear God, just the thought makes me wet.

I can tell my admission is just as unexpected to Riley, because his hand stills, and he makes a small noise in the back of his throat. I expect the next question will be *who*—who do I imagine is touching and teasing me like that?

That question doesn't come, and I'm grateful. Because I'm not ready to admit it's him.

But Riley says nothing. Instead, the fingers of one hand dip under the leather bustier, then roughly pinch my nipple. I cry out, my pussy clenching as sparks shoot through me, making me gasp with surprise. It wasn't a massive orgasm, but damned if I didn't just come.

"Oh, Christ, baby," he whispers. "I'm sorry."

I turn to face him, the sensation still lingering on me. "Sorry?"

He cups my face. "I promised you'd be safe with me. That everything in here would be consensual. I had no idea you'd come from nipple play. That you were so incredibly responsive."

"Is that bad?"

He tilts his head back and laughs, then seems to realize that he's drawn a bit of an audience now, too. "No," he assures me. "Not at all."

"Then don't apologize." I bite my lower lip, then tell him most of the truth. "It felt incredible." I keep the full truth to myself—that part of my reaction stemmed not from the touch, but by the fact that it was Riley doing the touching.

He tilts his head, and I see a question in his eyes. But I look away, unwilling to admit any more.

After a minute, he tugs on the collar. "We should continue the rounds. See, and be seen."

I nod, then stand and follow him around the room some more, my eyes taking it all in, my body on fire. I've never thought of myself as an exhibitionist, and I've never really considered being dominated. Most of the men I've slept with have been pretty vanilla. But I'm not a prude and I'm not ignorant. I've read my share of articles and books. But until I came here, I never put myself into the picture. Now, I see me in every one of these girls. More than that, starting with last night's dream, I see Riley standing over me.

Even more surprising, I realize that I don't mind his starring role in my fantasies.

My thoughts of him make me realize that he hasn't spoken since we left the bench, and I'm afraid that my unexpected reaction shocked him even more than it surprised me. "Riley?" I'm not sure he's heard me. I'm behind him, so I can't see his face. But then he stops and turns, his gaze skimming over me, making my entire body crackle with desire.

"What else?" he asks. "What else do you see that you like?"

The question makes me feel exposed, and I almost refuse to answer. After all, I've already shared way more with him than I'd planned. And yet I can't deny that this evening is turning into a journey of self-awareness. Including the awareness that for better or for worse, I want Riley Blade's hands on me again. And, yeah, I want a hell of a lot more than that, too.

"Tell me," he urges, coming to stand behind me. Once again, his hands go to my shoulders. He pulls me against him so that I feel his bare abs against my shoulders and the press of his erection against my lower back. His teeth nip the curve of my ear, and his voice slides over me, as sensual as warm honey. "Tell me," he repeats as his fingers move lightly over my breast, coming to a halt just beneath the edge of the bodice. "Tell me, and you'll get a reward."

"Riley—"

"Sir," he corrects. "Or Master. And there are punishments for girls who don't do as they're told."

I tremble in his arms, more aroused than I can ever remember being. "Yes, sir," I say, and feel one of his hands slip around to my lower back.

"Your safe word is pineapple," he tells me. "Now go on. What else in this room turns you on?"

I'm tempted to say simply *you*. But I know that's not what he means. So instead I tell him the truth. "I don't see them anymore."

"No? Well, that's an honest answer at least." His hand slides into my bodice, his fingertips brushing my nipple.

I bite my lower lip as he continues to speak. "Where were they before?"

"There." I nod toward the far side of the room and a simple straight-back chair.

He tugs on the back zipper of my leather pants, and I whimper. Not in protest, but in need.

"What were they doing?" he asks, rewarding my honestly by taking my nipple between his fingers and tweaking it, just rough enough to hurt. Just intense enough to make my knees go weak. "Tell me, baby. Tell me what you saw that you liked."

"He—he put her over his knee."

"Did he?" The zipper comes down a bit more. The fingers tighten on my nipple. And my breath comes in ragged, wild gasps. "What did he do next?"

Zip.

"He spanked her," I say.

His hand slides into the leather, his palm cupping my ass as his fingers curve beneath my legs to find my core.

I hear his sharp intake of breath as he realizes just how wet I am—how turned on he's making me, this place is making me.

And, yes, how turned on my revelations about my own desires are making me.

"Sir," I beg, and he groans as if in approval, then thrusts two fingers inside me.

"Is that what you want?" he asks, thrusting deeper as I try to surreptitiously grind down on him. And when he withdraws his fingers and starts to tease my clit, I'm pretty sure I'm going to lose my mind. "Do you want me to spank you until your ass is red and tingles, then finger you until you come? Do you want me to take you over my knee right now, your beautiful ass bared for all these people?"

Yes. Oh, please, yes. But I can't say the words. Instead I shake my head.

"Don't lie to me, baby," he murmurs. "Is it me? Do you want someone else's hand on your ass?"

"*No.*"

"Good." His finger strokes my clit again and I shift my hips, wanting to increase the sensation. I look around, trying to see if anyone is watching us, but no one seems to notice us at all. As far as anyone in this room is concerned, we're standing close together watching the scenes unfolding in front of us. Riley, I realize, doesn't seem out of place at all.

"Do you come to places like this often?"

"Would that bother you?"

I shake my head. "You know what to do. That makes me feel safe. I was just…curious," I say, the word true on so many different levels.

He brushes a kiss over the top of my head. "I'm glad. And yes, I come to places like this often, but I come mostly for work."

I note the *mostly*. "What do you mean?"

"I've been undercover at several clubs, and I've spent a lot of time at Sanctum."

I don't know what Sanctum is, but I assume it's another club. "So you're not, um, a real Dom."

He chuckles, and the sound ripples through me, setting off a flurry of sensual sparks.

"Today I am. Today, I'm your Dom."

"Oh." I lick my lips. "You mean because we're here pretending. Looking." I know I'm pushing the limit here. That I'm playing with fire. But that's okay. After all, I've already decided that I want to get burned.

There's a pause, then I feel his breath tickle the back of my neck. "No, baby. That's not what I mean."

I close my eyes and draw in a breath, his answer turning me on more than I anticipated it would. "What do you mean?"

"I think that's enough questions from you," he says, the hard edge to his voice letting me know that he's done talking about being a Dom. Now, he's just going to show me. "Tell me, baby. Have you ever been spanked?"

I consider not answering, but the time for game playing has passed. "No."

"Why do you want it now?"

I don't know what to say. Part of me wants to be punished for liking this more than I should. Part of me is simply curious.

But it's more than that. I like knowing that I'd be submitting to him even as I'm giving him a gift. Because I heard the arousal in his voice, and I know that the idea of spanking me turns him on, too.

"Maybe I don't know how to tell you," I admit. Then I add boldly, "Maybe you should punish me."

For an instant, his finger stills on my pussy, the hesitation so small that it would be imperceptible were I not so attuned to this man.

"Pineapple," he reminds me, then pulls his hands free of my clothes.

He takes the leash again and leads me to the chair, the leather clinging to my hips, but my bare ass exposed by the still-open zipper.

He sits, then nods and tells me to stand in front of him. "Unzip your bustier."

I widen my eyes at this unexpected turn of events. His mouth curves up, just a little smug. "I want what I want, too. Trust me. You'll like it."

I hesitate, but comply, pulling the zipper down to just above my navel. He reaches forward, then spreads the leather, revealing both my breasts. He shocks me then by reaching into his vest and pulling something out of an interior pocket. A chain with two small clamps on the ends.

Nipple clamps.

"Come closer," he orders, and though I move hesitantly, I comply.

"Will they hurt?" I ask, surprised to see him smile in response to the question.

"Good girl," he says. "You didn't try to avoid. You just asked a question. And the answer is a little. But then it will get better. And then, I promise, it will feel incredible. Okay?"

I nod, but he doesn't wait for my acquiescence. My nipples are hard as rocks, so it's easy enough for him to attach them. The clamps are adjustable, too, and I'm grateful that he doesn't have them on the tightest setting. Still, the initial pain is sharp, cutting down like a knife through me, and then settling into a fiery need that pools between my thighs.

"Dear God, Natasha," he says once the chain is attached to both my nipples. "Do you have any idea how hard I am just from looking at you?"

I lick my lips, my eyes dropping to his crotch. And yes, considering what I see, I really do have some idea. His erection is pressing so hard against the leather I know it must be painful, and I sigh as a wash of feminine power floods through me. I'm standing here with my nipples clamped, my breasts exposed, and my whole body leashed. I'm completely at his mercy—and yet in that moment I know that I'm the one with the power. The realization is heady, and I'm suddenly even more aware of the clamps on my sensitive nipples, not to mention the throbbing heat between my thighs.

There's another chain that comes off the middle of the steel links that connects my breasts, and I realize that its purpose is the same as my collar. A master could attach a leash, then lead his sub around by the tits.

The idea is wildly arousing, and once again I wonder what's come over me.

Riley.

I tell myself this is all about Riley, because it is. But not in a way that suggests recrimination. More like celebration. Being in this room— hell, even being exposed—is teaching me more about myself and my desires than I've been able to figure out in years of dating men who had no more allure to me than the first guy to take me to a high school football game. Sweet enough, but entirely lacking in chemistry.

What I've missed—what I've craved—is a man willing to truly acknowledge my sexuality. To challenge me. And to hold up a mirror to my own hidden desires.

A man like Riley, who is even now ordering me to tug down my pants. "Then I want you over my knees," he adds.

I hesitate, only now fully realizing that a spanking means I have to bare my ass. I glance around and see that there are a few people standing a respectful distance away. They're watching our scene play out, and while my reasonable side insists that I should want to melt into the floor with mortification, the real me is actually turned on by the existence of the audience.

I comply and tug the pants down enough to expose my ass.

What I don't do is tug down my thong, too. Which means that the audience sees my bare cheeks, but not my waxed pussy. I catch Riley's eye, swallow, and position myself over his knee.

For a moment, he doesn't move, and I hold my breath, afraid he's going to make me stand up and pull down the thong, even though my ass is completely bared to him and anyone else who cares to look.

But he takes pity on me, gently cupping his hand over the curve of my rear and then stroking in gentle circles as he murmurs, "So lovely."

I close my eyes, relaxing under his ministrations. The chair is low enough that I'm comfortable in this position, and I moan slightly in anticipation and longing when he says, "You were naughty not to remove your thong. For that, you'll need to be punished."

He rubs my ass, and then I feel the first sting of his palm on my tender skin. I gasp, the hot prickles of pain like tiny electric shocks. I feel drunk. On submission. On exhibition. On this wild new sensuality that is coursing through me, the explosion of flowers from a garden I didn't even realize I'd planted during my walk through this place with Lyle and Matthew.

A garden that only Riley could make bloom.

His hand comes down on my ass again, and I draw a tremulous breath, imagining the red rising on my ass. *A garden, all right,* I think. *A rose garden.*

He spanks me eight more times, rubbing my tender skin gently with each stroke. And when he's done, he opens a small bottle that is sitting in a square storage area in the arm of the chair, then spreads a soothing oil over my sore flesh before sliding his hand down over the curve of my ass to find my core.

I'm so wet and slick I'm dripping, and I whimper as his hand brushes my core, my pussy clenching with the desire to be fucked. His fingertip teases my clit, and though my mind says that I don't want to explode in front of these people, I can't stop myself. I writhe against his hand, seeking pleasure—seeking *Riley*. Harder and faster until, oh, dear God, I can't hold back any more. The orgasm barrels down over me, ripping me into a million pieces until, finally, I come back to myself, limp and sated over the legs of this man who's shown me more in one night than I could ever have dreamed.

"Come on," he says gently, carefully adjusting my pants and zipping me back up. "We need to go."

"Go? Why?" My entire body is on fire. I don't want to go. I want more.

"Because I need to be inside you, and you're not ready for me to fuck you in public."

"Oh." I swallow, desperately wanting to be home now, but at the same time remembering why we came in the first place. "Do—do you think he noticed us? My stalker, I mean."

One of his brows lifts. "Why don't we make sure of it? Why don't I show off my beautiful sub?"

I meet his eyes, then realize what he means. I swallow, but I don't protest. And I manage to hold my head up high as he leads me toward the exit on my leash, my bodice still wide open, my breasts completely exposed and dressed up in the fancy nipple clamps with the thin silvery chain.

Riley pauses when we reach the door that leads to the first room. The one that is really just a bar with snacks and virgin drinks. "I'm going to take you through like this," he says.

I press my lips tight together. Not in silent protest of what he's told me, but because I'm afraid that otherwise I'll say *pineapple*. And the truth is, I really don't want to. I want to do this. I want to *feel* it.

He's taken me this far. I want all of it.

He hesitates long enough to allow me to protest, and when I don't, he takes me the rest of the way through. Heads turn as I walk behind him, and while part of me trembles with the excitement of being on display, another part of me wonders if my stalker is in the crowd. If, perhaps, this will push him to move again. And if, just maybe, that by taking this risk I've paved the way to catching him.

When we reach the door to the reception area, Riley pulls me close, then takes my mouth in his. It's a long, deep, bone-melting kiss, and I press against him, realizing that this is what I've been wanting. Craving. And, yes, what I've been needing. Not the kiss, but the man. A man I tried to push away, but who was stubborn and pushy enough to—thank God—slide back into my life.

When he finally breaks the kiss, we're both breathing hard, and I see my desire reflected back at me. He gently zips up the bodice over the clamps, chuckling at my look of confusion.

"I meant to take them off of you earlier," he said. "To be honest, I was so damn turned on by how responsive you were to my hand on your ass, I completely forgot."

I bite my lower lip. "Why not just take them off now?" It's not hurting anymore—more like a pleasurable, intense sensation—but it's also somewhat awkward under the tight leather bustier.

But he just shakes his head. "Trust me," he says. And since I do, I remain quiet.

When we reach the car, he tells the driver to return to my house, then raises the privacy screen. "You liked that," he says, and I know he's talking about the whole experience. The entire night.

I don't pretend to misunderstand. "Yes," I admit.

"Tell me why."

I consider the question. "Because it felt naughty, and I've never really been naughty. And it felt safe, because I knew you were protecting me."

He gently cups my face. "That's why I'm here. To protect you."

I lick my lips, not sure I should say what's on my mind.

He seems to read my thoughts, though, because all he says is, "Tell me."

"It's just that I didn't mean that you were protecting me from my stalker. I know that's why we came, but to be honest, I forgot about him most of the time." I draw in a breath for courage. "I meant that it felt like you were protecting me from the world."

I look at him from under my lashes, afraid I've admitted too much. But I see only pleasure reflected on his face.

"That's all I've ever wanted, Natasha. And it kills me to know that most of the time when you look at me, you don't feel protected. You feel sad or afraid. I don't like that seeing me reminds you of all the horrible things that are out there in the world."

"Riley…" I choke on the emotion that clogs my throat. He's talking about the night my father died, and he's right. That's the burden I've forced on him all these years.

But maybe—just maybe—tonight has helped me move past that.

"I'm sorry for that," I say honestly. "But I know you understand how I feel. I know, because you do the same thing."

His brows rise. "I don't think so."

"Yes," I insist. "You do. You see this city and you think only of the bad things. You run from it because it's stained with all the memories you want to leave behind."

His eyes widen almost imperceptibly, and I realize he gets it. And knowing that I've given him a new perspective makes me feel powerful. More than that, I want to show him that my perspective on him has changed, too. Not just in the club, but out here in the world. Yes, he reminds me of my father. Yes, he reminds me of that night. But that's not all there is to Riley Blade, and I see a lot more of him now than just those memories that I'd attached to him in my mind.

With a playful little smile, I move onto the wide floorboard, then kneel in front of him.

His brows rise, but he doesn't say anything.

I put my hands on his knees. "I like being your submissive," I say.

His lips twitch. "Do you?"

I nod. "But now it's my turn to take charge."

"Is that so?"

I nod. "You need good memories of this town, Riley." I glance pointedly at his cock. "I think it's time I gave you some."

Chapter Seven

Riley was pretty damn sure that he'd never seen anything more erotic than Tasha's pink tongue licking his rock-hard cock. Good God, the woman surprised him. First in the club, when her combination of open trust and radiant curiosity had almost pushed him over the edge so many times. And now this, when she'd gathered the courage to turn the tables on him in the most delicious way possible—and still managed to be submissive even in the act of taking control.

She fascinated him. Aroused him.

Hell, she amazed him.

He'd been almost certain that she was submissive by nature. Not because she was subservient in her professional life—on the contrary, he'd seen how much control and responsibility she shouldered in her job with Lyle—but because the burden of that responsibility made him believe she'd fall willingly and gracefully into a submissive role.

She was a woman who needed to let go and give herself over to pleasure in order to learn just how much power she truly had. Because God knew, she held absolute power over Riley. For that matter, he thought, she'd wielded that power for years without ever even knowing it.

So yes, under the right circumstances he could imagine her collared and leashed in a club. He'd imagined that very thing more times than he'd liked to count.

What he hadn't expected was for his theory about her deeper nature to be proven right so quickly and dramatically, and the trust that she had lain at his feet humbled and amazed him.

And speaking of surprise…

He groaned, his eyes rolling back as she shifted position, going from licking him like a lollipop to closing her entire mouth on his cock and taking him deep. With one hand, he reached up and pressed against the roof of the car for leverage. With the other, he fisted her hair, stealing some of the control back as she worked his cock, taking him closer and closer to the edge.

"Touch yourself," he groaned. "Come on, baby. Slide your fingers between your legs and play with that sweet pussy. I'm so damn close, and I want you to come with me."

She made a raw, feral sound, then moved the hand that had been on the seat to give her leverage. He couldn't see that low, but as her other hand tightened at the base of his shaft, he was certain that she'd obeyed. Her sucking became wilder, filled now with the dual need of giving and taking pleasure. And the wild, animal noises she was making had the effect of pushing him right to the edge.

He held on, trying to hold back. Wanting her to come with him, but also wanting to hover at the edge for as long as possible. But soon he had no choice, and he let himself go, keeping his eyes open as he shattered, emptying himself in her sweet, sweet mouth. Watching as she took it all, her eyes opening as he finished to reveal a wild heat and something that looked like pride.

God, he loved her. More than that, he realized, he'd always loved her.

And now, as she teetered on that precipice, too, he bent forward and unzipped her bustier, then pulled hard on the middle of the chain, tugging both clamps off her nipples.

She cried out, a throaty moan made up of pleasure and pain as the blood rushed back to her nipples even as her fingers on her clit pushed her that final distance over the edge.

Her eyes were on him, but he could tell that it wasn't him she was seeing—it was light, stars, the expanse of the universe. And when he pulled her back up on to the seat beside him, she curled against him, and murmured only two words. "So good."

Content, he stroked her hair, letting her doze until they turned onto her street.

"We're here," he said softly, smiling as she blinked up at him.

"That wasn't fair, you know. I was supposed to be the one treating you."

"Not fair that we treated each other?"

"I think you destroyed me," she murmured. "In the best possible way, of course."

"You're welcome," he said, making her grin.

The car pulled into the driveway and the driver killed the engine. She slid down again, her head in his lap. "Can't we just stay here? Like maybe forever?"

He was tempted. That was damn sure. "Warm bed, baby," he said. "And if you're a very good girl, I'll make you a cup of cocoa before we go to sleep."

She tilted her head, her lips quirking as her brow lifted in mock incredulity. "Are you saying I wasn't already a good girl?"

He laughed—oh, yeah. He absolutely adored her.

As they waited for the driver to come around, Riley looked out the window, then frowned. "Nat," he said, his eyes on the big blob of orange fur sitting on the front porch. "I thought your cat stayed indoors."

"What?" She sprang up, all signs of exhaustion fading. "Pumpkin!"

She practically leapt over him and had the door open even before the driver reached it. He saw her zip up her bustier and her pants as she ran, then snatch up the cat and hug it close.

Riley was only steps behind her, and when she moved onto the porch as if to push the cracked front door fully open, he called out sharply for her to wait.

Her eyes went wide as the implications of her cat being outside and the door being open finally broke through her concern for Pumpkin.

Riley's rental car was in the drive, and he hurried to it, then retrieved the small Ruger he'd borrowed from Hunter from the glove box. He knew he couldn't take it into the club, so he hadn't even tried. But he was damn well keeping the thing on his person from now on.

With the gun at the ready, he returned through the door, then peered inside the house through the crack. The interior mat had been shifted onto the threshold, ensuring that the door couldn't close properly. More important, a chalkboard topped the mat. A simple one like the kind found in craft stores.

One word was neatly printed on it in pink chalk: *CHEATER*

Chapter Eight

I sit on my couch, a soft blanket wrapped around me, both for warmth and to hide the leather bustier from the gaggle of cops who have descended on my house. Not that I begrudge them being there—I want them to do whatever they can to find the asshole who's toying with me.

Riley has taken charge, and even though this is my house and I'm more than capable of watching out for it and myself, I let him. The truth is, I'm exhausted and I'm scared. It was one thing getting creepy notes. It's something else altogether to have someone inside my house. Someone who may or may not have intentionally put my cat out. My sweet Pumpkin who never harmed anyone and is far too pampered a kitty now to survive on LA's dangerous busy streets.

Fuck with me, and it may take me a while to get my ire up.

Fuck with my cat, and you're dead meat from the get-go.

After what seems like forever, most of the cops are gone, and Riley comes to me, then pulls me to my feet. "Why don't you go wait for me in the bedroom? I think I saw Pumpkin run hide in there, and she probably needs you."

"Maybe I need you," I say, then hate myself for sounding scared and needy.

Riley just kisses the corner of my mouth. "I'll be right here. But I want to finish up with Detective Garrison and check the work on the new locks. Stay if you want. I just thought you might like to get away from the insanity."

I nod. The truth is, he's right. "Thanks for taking care of this."

"I think we had this conversation earlier," he reminds me. "As long as you let me, I'll always take care of you. And frankly, I'll do it even if you protest."

The last part earns him a smile, even though we both know he's not joking. And I think it's that last little reminder of how much he cares that gives me the strength to leave him in charge of my domain and escape into the safety of my bedroom.

I'm not sure how long I'm in there, sitting on the edge of the bed petting Pumpkin before Riley comes back. All I do know is that when the door finally clicks open, the cat scrambles off my lap and races under the bed, only the orange tip of her tail showing.

"She going to be okay?"

Despite everything, I laugh. For over an hour, he's been overseeing the cops and the locksmith, doing everything in his power to make me feel safe and secure in my own house. Now, he's standing in the doorway wearing leather, his broad shoulders filling the frame, looking so damn tough he could be an action hero.

And what is he concerned about? The mental health and well-being of my cat.

"What?" he asks as my laughter ratchets up a notch.

"You," I say, smiling so wide it hurts. "Just...thank you."

He crosses to me, then sits on the bed and pulls me into his lap. "For what?"

I snuggle close, both content and amazed at how right it feels to be in his arms. "For taking care of me. For watching out for me. For tonight."

"Tonight," he repeats.

I nod, then shift on his lap so that I'm straddling him. "Every single thing about tonight," I say huskily as his cock stiffens beneath me. "Except the part where we got off track."

"Off track," he says, and I hear a welcome note of humor in his voice. "That's one way of putting it." He traces a finger over my collarbone and then lower over the swell of my breast. "I seem to recall we had very specific plans for when we reached your house tonight."

"Did we?" I tease as he unzips my bustier, then tosses it onto the floor.

"I seem to recall promising some very specific things," he continues, reaching back to unzip my pants. "Like, for example, fucking you senseless."

"Oh," I say, my tender nipples tightening again, the sensation wildly enticing.

"It's ridiculously late," he says, gently sliding me off his lap so that I'm standing in front of him. "But I have to have you. Tell me if you want me to stop," he adds as he falls to his knees and peels the pants and my thong down my legs. "Because, baby, right now I can't think about anything else but being inside you," he says, then licks my very sensitive pussy, sending a current of electricity racing through me.

"Riley…" It's the only word I conjure, but it's enough. My feet are already bare, and I kick out of the last of the leather pants as he leads me back to the bed, then lays me out naked.

He stands beside me, then shrugs off the black leather vest and lets it fall to the ground. I swallow, wondering if I'll ever get used to the beauty of this man. The strength and power he exudes.

Wondering if I'll ever stop craving him and knowing that I won't. Hell, that I don't want to.

For so long, I'd denied myself this man, and now I can barely remember why. He's blown through my defenses in record time and settled himself firmly in the Riley-shaped place in my heart that's been waiting for him for years.

He meets my eyes, his grin crooked and cocky, as if he knows what I'm thinking. As if he understands how much I want him. All of him.

Then his hand goes to his fly, and I actually whimper. After everything we've done together, I realize with surprise that I haven't actually seen him naked. And I hold my breath as he pulls the leather down. Since he's gone commando, his cock springs free, hard and thick and huge.

Without thinking, I reach for him, but he just steps away from my fingers, his grin suggesting that he knows he's tormenting me.

I expect him to get onto the bed, but first he grabs up the vest. I see him reach into a slim pocket on the inside, and then toss something onto the bedside table. I glance over and see a packet of condoms. "Boy Scout," he says, making me laugh.

Then he gets onto the bed and straddles me. It's almost three in the morning, and I've been through a lot, but the moment his skin touches mine, all traces of exhaustion leave me, overcome by the sheer power of this man.

"I want to hold you," he tells me. "I want to fall asleep with you in my arms. But first, I have to be inside you."

"Yes," I whisper. "Oh, dear God, yes."

We move together, slow and easy. Fingers touching. Mouths teasing. Our bodies fit perfectly, and he takes me on my back, my knees bent up to my chest so that he can go deep, his rhythmic thrusts filling me and making the bed shake with the motion. His body covers me, and his cock fills me, and as we move together, I lose my sense of self. We're one, a unit, and I can't tell where he begins and I end. Even when he starts to come, I feel the ripples of his release break through me, taking me over the edge as well.

And when he calls out, his voice a raw, guttural groan, for me to go over with him, I break apart, my body answering his command without question, shattering with him, and then coming back together in his arms.

We stay like that, him on top of me, looking into each other's eyes for what feels like an eternity. They say that the eyes are the windows to the soul, and I believe it. Because as I look deep into Riley's dark eyes, I know that I'm seeing the full measure of the man. More than that, I know that I love him. I think I always have.

What I don't know is if he feels the same way. Or, if he does, how we can possibly make this work.

Those same thoughts swirl in my head as we spoon together, my back to his chest, as sleep creeps up on us.

I, however, fight it back. It's not sleep I want. It's Riley. It's a future. And to get there, we have to reconcile the past.

I take a deep breath, then exhale, hoping he hasn't drifted off already. "About before," I say. "The years before, not earlier today."

"Yes?" His voice is tired, but I know I have his attention.

"It's not just that seeing you made me remember my father. That's not the only reason I pushed you away."

"Wasn't it?"

"No. It's that I didn't think that I could stand the strain of knowing I might lose you at any minute the same way I lost him." My voice is tight with emotion, and I exhale noisily. "But it doesn't matter anyway, does it? Because you don't like this city. And once you catch my stalker, you're going to leave. Aren't you?"

He's silent for a moment, then he says, "Is that what you want?"

I lick my lips, suddenly unsure. I can't imagine living with that fear every day. I don't know how my mother did it. She died of complications following surgery three years before my father did. I sometimes wonder if in some way that was a relief to her. Or is it just simply proof that worrying about the obvious dangers is foolish, because the unexpected ones will get you anyway?

"I don't know," I say after a moment, realizing I haven't answered his question. But how can I? I want the man. But I also want certainty and safety. Or at least as much certainty as is humanly possible.

"You love this town," he says after a moment.

"I do." I want to turn and see his eyes, but I don't. These are things we've never talked about, and they're important. And I don't want to stop—or risk doing anything that makes him stop. "But it's mostly my job that I love," I admit.

"Lyle?"

"Partly. Working for him is great. But I truly love Hollywood. If they moved the heart of the film industry somewhere else, I'd follow." I draw in a breath, and then tell him the real truth. "I want to be part of making happy endings," I admit. "I can't act or produce or direct or any of that. But I can help. I can make a difference for the ones who craft the stories, and that matters."

"It does," he agrees.

"The stories matter, too. To the public, sure, but also to me. I need to be part of the fairy tale. Honestly, even though I was born in LA, I sought out Hollywood. I came to it because it was my due. Because in my real world, when Cinderella lost her shoe, it ended up tossed in a junk heap. And Sleeping Beauty got tetanus from that damn needle prick."

I take a breath. "I wanted to help make happily ever afters, and if I couldn't do it in real life, then I'd help do it on the screen in whatever way I could wrangle."

"I get that," he says. "There's not much that's more important than making your own happy ending."

I smile, more pleased than I'd anticipated that he seems to understand why my work, which probably looks to someone on the outside like something I could do for any exec in any industry, is important to me.

"What about you?" I ask. "How'd you end up on a SWAT team with my dad? Were you following in your own father's footsteps?"

"No," he says. "Honestly, I don't know why. I just know that it's what I've always wanted. I like order. I appreciate respect. And I like to live in a world where there are rules. You break them sometimes, sure. But for the most part, the idea is to mold a world that makes sense. That's sane and safe." I feel him shrug. "I guess the bottom line is that I want to help people. And by doing that I go a little ways toward making the world that I want to live in."

"That makes sense," I say.

"Bottom line, I'm selfish."

I laugh. "Bottom line, you're one of the best men I know. You didn't have to help me. You could be off in China right now."

"But I'm not," he says. "I'm here right now. And at least for the moment, I'm not going anywhere."

I sigh, then I break my own rule and turn to face him. "Hold me," I say. "Hold me, and then find me in your dreams."

Chapter Nine

Thank God for friends, Riley thought as he shook Zac Tyson's hand. *And for Ian Taggart.*

"Not sure how much help I can be," the burly man with the shaved head and Chicago Cubs T-shirt said as he greeted Riley in the now-deserted reception area. "But if Taggart says you deserve the open door policy, then you got it, my friend."

"Appreciate it." Riley had texted Big Tag with a quick and dirty summary of the situation, then asked Tag to reach out to Jared for an intro to The Firehouse's owners so that he could get access to the security set-up. Instead, Tag had gone one step further and hooked Riley up with the club's security guru. Apparently Zac had done some surveillance work for Taggart. Which Riley probably should have anticipated. Never underestimate Ian Fucking Taggart, after all.

Riley and Nat had slept until eight, when Pumpkin had decided she was hungry and had taken to batting Riley's face until he woke up. He and the cat had bonded over tuna and coffee, and then he'd returned to the bedroom where he'd very methodically kissed his Sleeping Beauty awake.

They'd made love in the shower, after which she'd pulled together a breakfast of eggs and toast. The whole morning had felt ridiculously, wonderfully domestic, especially after the heated decadence of the night before. And Riley, who never stayed over at a woman's house, had sat in the chair watching her cook, all the while thinking that he could get used to that.

The text had come in while they were eating, and since the only time Zac had available that morning was when Nat needed to be on a conference call, they'd decided he'd go by himself.

He saw her safely to the condo office, double-checked to make sure the elevator and door security were working properly, then told her not to go out for any reason.

With her assurance ringing in his ear, he'd headed downtown to The Firehouse and his meeting with Zac.

"We only have security in this area," Zac said, a sweep of his arm encompassing the reception area, where members checked in before being admitted through to the bar. "And it's not as if we require them to look straight into a camera before entering," he says.

"Do you scan membership cards upon entry?"

"No," Zac said. "Our members appreciate the *fact* of membership, but once they're in the club, they don't want to feel like they're flashing a bus pass. And, to be honest, some of our members are well-known celebrities. Without an entrance scan, they have deniability."

"Sure, I joined," Riley said. "But it was just as a joke. I never actually went there."

"Exactly," Zac nodded "And if there's no entrance scan, who's to say otherwise?"

"That camera." Riley pointed to the two high-mounted—but camouflaged—security cameras.

"Good eye, but you see the problem. If a client keeps his head down or wears a mask or sunglasses, any identification will be a problem."

Riley nodded. The man was right. "Gotta give it a shot."

"Tag said you're looking for a stalker."

"Someone's been harassing my girlfriend." And, dammit, she *was* his girlfriend whether she knew it yet or not. "I intend to put a stop to it."

"You think she picked up the stalker here." He nodded, not waiting for Riley's answer. "I like to think that kind of element isn't among our membership, but I also can't deny that it's possible." He met Riley's eyes. "She's the one who came with Holt on that research walk-through, you said?" He flipped through a calendar open on the main desk. "Let's take a look at the security feed and see who we see."

"Appreciate it," Riley said, though he was feeling significantly less appreciative four hours later after reviewing the tapes from the first night and then comparing it to the previous night, looking for overlap since the stalker seemed to know she'd been at the club last night. Though even that wasn't certain. It may have simply been coincidence that the stalker had accused her of cheating.

Riley didn't think so. More likely the stalker saw her with Riley—and was angry for her infidelity.

No one, however, stood out as having come twice. He did clearly see a gray-haired man with a cane on the arm of a masked woman with a mole on her upper lip. Not likely that a man who brought his own sub would be a stalker, but anything was possible, and he asked Zac to find out the man's name. He saw five other men whom he believed showed up again on the second day, but the images weren't sufficient to be certain.

"Sorry not to be more help," Zac said. "But I'll make you some prints and see what I can find out about our gray-haired friend. And I'll try to get you some names on those five. I think you're right. They each came on the second night, too. Especially this one." He backed up the footage, then focused on a man with broad shoulders and dark hair that curled just past his ears. "See that?" He pointed to a shadow on the back of the man's neck. "I don't think it's a shadow."

"A tattoo?"

"On his shoulder," Zac said. "I think the shadow is the edge of the ink work."

"You may be right," Riley said. "Good eye."

"Gives us a little more to go on," Zac said, and Riley nodded, though he thought Zac's optimism might be misplaced. And he told as much to Natasha when he arrived at the condo that afternoon.

She greeted him at the door with a bright smile, then slid into his arms the moment he shut the door behind him. He drew her close, then lost himself in a slow, lingering kiss. A simple greeting, maybe, but it meant so much, including revealing just how far Tasha had come.

And, damn, but he could get used to this.

"Did you learn anything?" she asked, but he only shook his head. "A few leads, maybe. I'll give you the rundown when we get to your house. I dropped a few things off earlier."

Her brows rose. "Did you? Like what?"

He thought of the items he'd picked up from both the grocery store and the hardware store. But all he did was smile. "That," he said, "is my little surprise."

Chapter Ten

"I don't think I've noticed any of these people," I say, flipping through the printouts that Riley handed me as soon as we got into his rented BMW. He'd insisted we take my car in to have the hood repainted. And, frankly, I was fine with erasing that particular memory. "You really think one of these men is my stalker?"

"I think the odds are good, but honestly the position of the security camera makes it hard to compare guests across the course of days. Zac agrees that the setup is lame—he didn't install the system and only started working there a few months ago."

"So now that he knows, he'll fix it." I lift a shoulder. "Too late for me, but that should help someone else."

"Not necessarily too late for you," Riley says. "Zac's going to try to get me names, and we'll see what we see. Oh, I do know that we can rule our gray-haired suspect out. The one with the younger woman on his arm."

"Yeah? How do you know that?"

"Zac texted as I was setting up the house earlier. He visits the club at least four times each week, often brings a guest, and left yesterday about an hour after he arrived because he got a call that his daughter was in labor. The girl who works the door said he was positively beaming when he left, and I checked with the hospital. He went straight to Cedars and was there through the night until his grandson was born this morning."

"A happy ending, at least," I say, my mind shifting to Aly as I make a mental note to call and update her. After all, a lot's happened in a short time.

I lean back in the leather seat, then frown as I recall our conversation. "What do you mean by setting up the house? My house?" I turn to face him. "What did you do?"

"Hopefully something you'll like. Don't worry. Nothing too invasive. Just one trip to Home Depot and I was good to go."

I narrow my eyes. He's teasing me, of course. I'm guessing he either installed an alarm system or he bought me flowers. Either way, I'm good.

As it turns out, though, I'm not good enough. Because when we get home, I realize I'm completely off the mark. There is no alarm system—although he tells me that he did talk to Ryan Hunter about finding someone to install one at cost—and my living and dining areas are entirely lacking in flowers.

"You were just pulling my chain," I say. "You haven't done a thing to my house. Unless…" I trail off, looking toward the kitchen. "Are you cooking me dinner?"

"Not exactly," he says.

"Hmmm." I'm still trying to get it out of him when he grabs me from behind and spins me around, catching me in the circle of his arms. "Is this the surprise?" I murmur. "Because I like this very much."

"Kissing you shouldn't be a surprise," he says. "It should be an everyday occurrence."

As if to prove it, he presses me against the wall, cages me in his arms, and kisses me so thoroughly my legs barely manage to keep me upright.

"No, the surprise has more to do with something you saw at the club. Something that intrigued you."

"Oh." My body fires simply from the mention of the club, but the truth is that I still haven't got a clue. Because, frankly, the whole damn place intrigued me. "So are we going back tonight?"

He shakes his head. "I think one day away is a good policy. We'll see if there's any incidents tonight or tomorrow. If not, that only helps establish the connection to the club."

"I get that," I say. "But you said—"

He cuts me off with a chuckle. "I never said we were going to the club. Doesn't mean the club can't come to you."

Now I'm more confused than ever, but I decide to just give up and let him lead.

"So you trust me," he says, and I nod. Because I do. I trust this man with all of me. My heart. My body. Hell, I'd even trust him with my life.

"Good," he says, then looks me up and down. When his eyes meet mine again, I see the change in him. As if he's taking on a persona and is gathering power around him. There's command in his posture and control in his eyes, and just looking at him makes me weak with desire and wet with longing.

"Take off your clothes, Natasha."

We're still in the entrance hall, but I don't even hesitate. I step out of my shoes, then strip off my blouse and bra, then my slacks and underwear. Then I stand naked in front of him, not shy this time, but aroused and curious, my entire body humming with anticipation.

"Oh, baby," he says, his eyes dipping to my nipples, already painfully tight from my arousal. "You want me. More than that, you want whatever I have planned for you."

"Yes," I say.

"Even without knowing what it is."

"Yes."

He steps in front of me, then takes my hand and presses it over his erection, straining against his jeans. "Do you have any idea how hard that makes me?"

I meet his eyes, then glance down to my hand. "I do now."

He chuckles, then leads me to the far side of the living room where there is a sliding glass door that looks out over my lush, plant-filled backyard.

The curtains are open, but I know that the odds are slim that someone is looking in. Still, it's a possibility, and I have to force myself not to ask him to close the drapes.

The thought sends my eyes darting to the track, and that's when I notice the hardware on the ceiling. Two giant hooks. And when I look down, I see more on the ground.

I look to Riley in confusion.

"The cross," he said. "You wanted to try it. But not where everyone could see you."

I gasp as a wave of red hot desire crashes over me, making me so wet I feel the slickness on my thighs. And it's not just the thought of being bound like that, teased like that. It's the realization that he remembered—and that he took the time to bring me this experience in a way that stayed inside my comfort zone.

"Riley…"

He presses a finger over my lips, then leads me to the glass door. It takes some machinations, but soon I'm standing with my arms and legs spread, as if forming an X. He has soft cuffs on my ankles and wrists and they are each attached to the hooks with a mechanism that he assures me provides for a quick release. My back is to the glass, and the drapes are open. And though I really, *really* don't think anyone is looking, some small part of me has to acknowledge that the possibility adds to the excitement.

When he comes forward, he has a single ostrich feather in his hand. "Close your eyes," he orders, and when I comply, he strokes my body with the feather, paying special attention to my nipples, my neck, my inner thighs, and my sex.

The teasing is merciless, the sensations as wild as he is relentless, and without thinking about it, I realize that I'm gyrating in my bindings, my hips moving as if that will provide some release.

"Christ, that's hot, baby. Do you know what you're doing to me?"

A memory rolls over me. The first time I saw him in the FBI office when I'd come to visit my dad. My certainty that one day he'd be mine. And then later—the morning of that horrible day—when he'd asked me out with those words. *Tasha,* he'd said. *Do you know what you do to me?*

I didn't then, but I do now. It's fire between us. It's heat and fire and life. It's passion.

And right now, it's driving me crazy.

When I hear the low thrum of the vibrator, I know it's about to get even crazier, and though I don't mean to, I actually whimper.

"You are so fucking sexy, Nat," he says, his palm caressing my ass. And before I even realize I've spoken, I say, "Call me Tasha."

His hand stills. "Are you sure?"

"It's who I am," I say. "Please, Riley. Call me Tasha, and make me come."

"*Tasha.*" My name is like a prayer. A curse. An incantation, and as if the name has conjured it, he brushes the vibrator lightly over my clit, playing me expertly until I'm bucking and begging, unable to truly escape this brutal, beautiful torment.

He doesn't, however, give me release. Just takes me to the edge and then pulls me back, so that by the time he releases me from the bindings and carries me to bed, I'm so wet, ready, and desperate that I don't even let him finish undressing. Instead, I take his hand and tug him onto the bed with me. Then I shove his jeans down just enough to free his beautiful cock, straddle him, and take him so fast and so deep that I not only forget my own name, I swear I glimpse heaven.

He clutches my hips, and I ride him hard, a second orgasm rolling through me when he comes hard and fast inside me. I cry out his name, then collapse, sated and satisfied, beside him.

"Dear God, Tasha." He's breathing hard, his voice raspy with passion. "You break me like no other woman."

I turn in his arms, my own breath ragged as I look deep into his eyes, wanting to see his soul. His secrets. "No," I say. "Not broken. I think we make each other whole."

Chapter Eleven

Matthew Holt frowned at the photos that Riley handed him. "Considering I spend half my life looking at casting photos, you'd think I'd be better with faces, but honestly, none of these look familiar. You say they were all at the club the night we went on the research visit?"

"They were. These are from that night's security feed."

"I'm sorry," Matthew said. He passed them back across his desk to Riley, accidentally shifting the placement of a framed photo in the process.

From where Riley was sitting, he could see that it was a group shot, and though he only got a quick glance, something about it set his senses tingling.

"Do you mind?" he asked, though the question was for form only. He already had the photo in his hand. Now that he was looking directly at it, though, nobody jumped out at him.

"Is something wrong?" Matthew asked.

"I'm not sure. There's something so…" He trailed off, shaking his head. "Where was this taken?"

"A company picnic," Matthew told him. "The woman in white is my ex-wife, but it's one of the few photos I have of my whole staff." He frowned. "I keep thinking I should Photoshop her out of the image."

Riley didn't respond. He was too busy looking at the woman with long dark hair and full red lips. Familiar lips.

He passed the photo to Matthew. "Who is this?" he asked as he stood and crossed to the giant dry erase board that covered the far wall of Matthew's office.

"Joanna Stein," he said. "She's one of my assistants."

"She a member of the club?"

Matthew's eyes widened. "Not as far as I know, but she went a few times with me."

"Interesting extracurricular to share with an employee."

"We went out socially a few times," Matthew admitted. "But after a while, I thought better of it. Told her that I couldn't date someone on my staff. But honestly, that was just an excuse. The truth is we didn't connect. She was too…"

He trailed off, obviously searching for a word.

"What?"

"I'm not sure how to describe it. I just felt that she focused on me—on us—too quickly. That she'd be clingy, except that's not right either. I guess I just had a bad feeling. Why? Surely you don't think Joanna knows who's stalking Natasha."

"She knows all right," Riley said, using the dry erase marker to draw a small mole above Joanna's lip. Then he passed the image back to Matthew. "She *is* the stalker. And I think you're the reason."

"Me?"

"You went to the club with Tasha. She saw you. And now she's pissed that you have a new girlfriend."

"Dear God."

"Is she here today? Can you call her into your office?"

"Of course." He pressed the intercom button. "Lisa, can you ask Joanna to step into my office?"

"I'm sorry, Mr. Holt. She's already left with your delivery."

"Delivery?" He met Riley's eyes. "What delivery?"

"The one for Mr. Tarpin. The additional research material for the erotic thriller. She's on her way to his office right now."

* * * *

I'm sitting on the floor with the laptop on the coffee table in front of the window and three boxes' worth of backlogged filing spread out around me. I'm determined to get through all of this before Lyle comes back, mostly because once he does return, all of this non-priority work will get pushed to the background.

But Lyle insists on keeping old call sheets, fan mail, reviews, articles, interviews, the whole nine yards. Some of it I can save directly into our digital filing system. But some of it—like the stuff in these boxes—has to be sorted and filed. Do I scan it? Or is it cool enough that years from now, Lyle might want the actual magazine? Like the first time he made the cover of *People*. That's a no-brainer. But what about the other two times? Scan or keep a hard copy?

I sit back, scowling, and am rescued from the whole decision-making conundrum by the chime on my phone that signals someone requesting access to the lobby and the elevator banks. I check the image on the app, then use the intercom feature to confirm that the arrival is the woman from Matthew Holt's office. Joanna, one of his assistants, had called earlier to say she wanted to run by some material for Lyle to review upon his return—a sheath of research material for the new project and a revised outline.

I'd mentioned the material in my morning call with Lyle, just to be sure that he didn't want me to have her send the stuff straight to him in Europe, but he'd said to go ahead and review it myself. "You're sure it's Joanna?"

"Pretty sure, why?"

"The last time I was in, he'd mentioned that he was considering letting her go. He either changed his mind or I'm thinking about a different assistant."

I remember the conversation as I wait for the elevator to bring her up to the thirtieth floor. If she is the woman that Matthew's thinking about firing, I can't help but feel sorry for her. It would suck to be on the chopping block and not even know it.

Moments later, there's a soft knock, and I climb to my feet and open the door to reveal a woman with short dark hair and bright red lipstick. "Hey, you must be Joanna. I'm Natasha. Come on in."

"Thanks." She glances around. "Great office."

I explain how it used to be Lyle's apartment. "Thus the awesome security."

"Yeah, I wish Matthew had that. It's a crazy world these days."

"Tell me about it," I say, though I don't elaborate. "Come on. I have a pot of coffee in the sitting area if you want some. Cream, sugar, these cool little chocolate stir sticks. It's my afternoon treat. Just ignore all the papers on the floor."

She follows me in, and I pour us both coffee while she explains what she brought over. "The BDSM research is really pretty interesting.

We can go over it if you want."

I shoot her a sideways glance, wondering if she's flirting with me. Because, honestly, I'm capable of reading research materials all on my own. But I decide I'm imagining things, because she's not even looking at me anymore. Instead, she's tapping her lip with the stir stick as she flips the pages in the folder. A nervous habit, I presume, but there's something so familiar about it, I start to think that maybe I have met her before. One day at Matthew's office, maybe?

I'm about to ask her if we've crossed paths before when my phone rings, the display announcing that it's Aly. "I'm really sorry," I say, grabbing my phone. "But it's my best friend, and she's pregnant."

"Oh, no worries." The stir stick has left a chocolate mark on her lip, which for some reason bothers me more than it should, but since the call has just connected, I don't mention that she needs to wipe it off.

"Hey," I say. "Listen, I've got someone in the office with me. I just answered to make sure you're okay."

"I'm totally fine. But I have a doctor's appointment later today and Ben can't drive me. Do you think you can?"

I glance toward Joanna, wondering how long she's going to stay. And then realize it doesn't matter. I can't drive her without a car. More than that, I wouldn't drive Aly even if my car wasn't in the shop. What if my stalker decided to upshift the action? No way am I putting Aly and the baby in the stalker's line of fire.

I'm about to tell her as much and suggest she call someone else, when the words catch in my throat as I notice her mole and realize where I've seen Joanna before—*She's the guest of the gray-haired man.*

And while that might be a completely freakish coincidence, as far as I'm concerned, that means that she's my stalker.

A woman. Why the hell had we never thought that the stalker was a woman?

I shove the question aside. Right now, that's really not important. The bigger questions are what does she want right now? How am I going to get out of here? And how the hell do I get in touch with Riley?

For the last, at least, I have an idea.

"That's so scary," I tell Aly, who makes a confused sound on the other end of the line as I barrel on. "You need to call them right now and tell them to send you the right blade. Honestly, someone could get hurt."

"What the hell?"

"I mean it," I say in a no-nonsense voice. "Call and chew those bastards out right now. Make them send you a new blade immediately because that old one is just going to hurt someone."

"I—Oh, shit. Right." She hangs up, and I continue talking.

"Good, you do that. And yeah, I can come over later. We can have virgin piña coladas and watch bad movies. See you later. Okay. Bye."

I hang up, certain that Joanna saw right through my ruse. But she's just sipping her coffee and appearing completely bored.

What if I'm wrong?

What if I've got this all wrong and Aly's calling Riley?

I draw in a breath, then let it out slowly. Better safe than sorry, right? And I'm certain that's what Riley would say.

But what should I do in the meantime? Is she dangerous? Do I try to get out of the apartment? Do I try to lock her in the pantry?

I decide to assume that she is dangerous. After all, stalkers stalk. Once they make actual contact, that can't be a good thing. And since I have no idea how to cajole her into the pantry—which actually does have a lock since we converted it into a vault—I decide that it makes the most sense to just get the hell out of dodge myself.

"I just realized this is heavy cream," I say, taking the cream pitcher and standing. "I'm going to go get some half-and-half."

"Oh, don't bother," she says, then lunges at me, knocking the table over and sending the coffee service and my phone flying as she catapults me backward onto the couch.

I struggle to sit up, only to find her pulling a long, thin knife from her bag and smiling at me as if we're just two friends at a cocktail party. "I'm fine with cream. What I really want to do is talk about how you're fucking my boyfriend. Because that's not the kind of thing one girl should do to another."

"Mr. Holt?" I say, even though I'm certain I can't talk myself out of this. "I'm not sleeping with him. I have a boyfriend. His name's Riley." It's true, I realize, and the thought of Riley strengthens my resolve.

"Don't you dare lie, you bitch."

"I'm not." I keep my voice low and level. "I wouldn't do that to you. I only want—"

She lunges, proving that all those long negotiation scenes in movies are just bullshit. I roll sideways and tumble off the couch, then kick up, knowing it won't stop her, but hoping it buys me a few seconds to get to my feet so I can race for the door.

It doesn't work. Yes, I manage to land my feet hard in her gut, sending her tumbling backward, but that's only after she sinks her knife into my thigh. I scramble backward, lightheaded from the pain and the sight of blood. But it's no use. She's already back on her feet. She's already coming toward me.

And because of the couch on one side of me and a heavy armchair a few feet from my head, there's no place that I can go.

Chapter Twelve

"Get the fuck out of the way, you lousy piece of shit." Riley slammed his hand onto the steering wheel, his horn blasting at the BMW in front of him, which of course had nowhere to go in this fucking bottleneck on Santa Monica Boulevard.

He growled and pressed redial on his phone, but once again he only got Tasha's voicemail. *Shit, shit, motherfucking shit.*

He laid on the horn again, not because it would do any good. Just because he was so wound up he'd probably kill somebody if he couldn't offload some of his fear and frustration.

Surely she's okay.

Surely she just has her phone on silent.

Finally—*finally*—the traffic moved enough to let him turn off this motherfucking road, and once he was clear, he floored it, then laid on the horn as he blew down surface streets as he zig-zagged in and out of traffic, stopping only when traffic patterns and red lights forced the issue.

He was at just such a light when his phone rang. He glanced at the Caller ID, saw it was Ian Taggart, and hit the button to connect the call.

"Why the hell aren't you in China?"

"Why the hell are you calling me? I'm in kind of a rush here. Some serious shit hitting the fan."

"So I've heard. I just got a call from some woman named Aly. Says she has a message for you from Natasha but didn't know how to reach you. But she remembered you work for me, and so she called the number on the website. Gotta love the modern world, huh?"

Oh, Christ. "What was the message?" His voice was tight, and he was working to hold back his fear.

"The girl just said that they were on the phone and all of a sudden Natasha told Aly that she needed to get a new blade. Said that since the words made no sense, she figured that was a code. A message for you."

Thank God for Allison McCray. Riley hadn't seen her in probably six years, but in that moment, she was his best friend in the whole damn world.

The light changed and he floored it into the intersection. "Do me a favor and call Detective Garrison for me. I talked to him already, so he should be en route, but tell him the situation I told him about has escalated. I'm on my way now. And for God's sake, Ian, tell them to hurry."

* * * *

There's crazy in Joanna's eyes as she lunges at me once again, leading with the knife. And though I may be trapped, I'm not giving up. It hurts like hell, but I thrust my legs up and out, catching her in the gut and giving me a few precious seconds to climb to my feet so that I can stumble out of here.

Except I *can't* climb to my feet. The wound is too bad, and as I try to rise, I stumble once more, then fall, smacking my head on the corner of the table in the process.

"He's mine," Joanna says, her words sounding like they are underwater. "He doesn't want you. He wants you to just go away."

My hand closes around the fallen coffee pot, and I force myself to think. To not give in to the pain in my head. I try to hurl it at her, but I have no strength, and it travels only inches.

Joanna laughs. "You should calm down." She strokes a finger over the blade of her razor-sharp knife, raising a thin layer of blood. "It will only hurt a little, then it will stop. As the blood leaves you, it will all stop. And then we'll both be fine. You see? It's all so simple."

Hell, yeah, it's simple. You're crazy. I blink, realizing I've only said the words in my head. The pain in my leg and the pain in my head are drawing me under, and I'm not even scared. I'm just lost and sad. *Riley.* I won't even have the chance to say good-bye to Riley.

Above me, Joanna's face contorts, and she lifts the knife at the same time I hear a loud crash from the far side of the room. I have no idea what it is—I'm on the floor, my vision blocked by the couch.

But the next thing I hear is a sharp crack, and then the knife clatters to the ground. For a moment, Joanna looks stunned. Then I see that her hand is a bloody mess.

Gunfire, I think, as my head pounds and my vision turns gray.

I fight to stay conscious. But it's hard, and things are moving so slowly. I have to stay awake though. I have to fight so she doesn't hurt me again. But it's hard—it's so damn hard.

And then I hear a feral yell, and as if in slow motion, someone leaps into view, knocking Joanna to the ground before turning his attention to me.

I try to smile, but I'm not sure I manage.

Riley.

He's here, and I'm safe.

And that's when I relax and let the gray pull me under into sleep.

* * * *

"I could have lost you," Riley says hours later as he carefully settles me into my bed. "I just found you again, and I could have lost you."

"But you didn't," I say. It's the same thing I've been saying for the last two hours—ever since I woke up in the condo as he'd held me, his muscles straining as he kept pressure on my leg while we waited for the police and paramedics. I reach out and clasp his hand. "You didn't lose me. You saved me."

"I sent Big Tag a text message from the hospital. I'm done. With Dallas. With all of it."

The words are clear enough, but they make no sense, and I decide that I must be woozier from the pain meds than I thought. The knife missed my femoral artery, thank goodness, but it was still a deep slash, and I now sport a lovely set of twelve stitches on my thigh and some even lovelier pain meds pumping through my veins.

"Ian Taggart," he says, obviously seeing my confusion. "My boss. I quit. I'm not going back to work."

That time I understand the words, but I'm still fuzzy on the meaning. "Why?"

His laugh is strangled, and when he cups my cheek and looks into my eyes, I see that the man looking back at me is just as wounded as I am. "Why? Because I can't leave you. Because I'm staying here."

My heart skitters, and I fear that the drugs and the pain have discombobulated my brain. Surely he's not saying what I think he's saying. Is he?

"You're not going back to Dallas?"

"No." He takes my hand, then kisses my fingertips. "I told you. I'm staying here."

"Oh." I lick my lips, barely daring to hope. "But you hate it here."

He studies my face, his expression tender. "I did. I've had a change of heart." He draws a breath. "I don't want to scare you by moving too fast, but I love you, Natasha Black, and I want a chance to make this work between us."

My chest tightens, and I can't speak through the tears of joy that are trying so desperately to escape.

"I figure I can consult on films and television. Lyle and Matthew can help me line up work. God knows this town makes enough action movies that I won't starve."

It takes a moment for those words to process, and when they do, I take his hand. "I can't... I don't think I can handle that. Knowing I pulled you away from something you love. I don't want you to resent me."

"I wouldn't."

"You might. But it's more than that. It's part of who you are. Just like it was part of who my dad was. And even though the worst happened to him, I wouldn't want to go back and change who he was. And I don't want to change who you are either."

His brows rise. "Are you saying you want me to call Tag and tell him I'm moving back to Dallas after all?"

I smack him lightly on the chest. "Don't you dare. But maybe you could tell him you're open to freelance? When he needs you? And you could even do freelance work for Ryan, too. And the Hollywood consulting. That should keep you busy. The rest of your time can be devoted to pleasuring me."

"Oh, can it?"

"Absolutely. In fact, you can start by kissing me."

"Anything you want," he says, then slides a hand under my neck as he rises over me, his mouth closing hot and gentle over mine, a kiss like making love slowly, lazily. A kiss that holds a promise of things to come, and when he pulls away, I regret the pain in my thigh and the exhaustion and drugs that weigh down my body. But at the same time, I know it doesn't matter. There will be so many more nights between us, and so very much to look forward to.

"I love you, Riley Blade."

"Oh, Tasha, I love you, too."

I sigh, deeply satisfied, then press my cheek to his bare chest. "We do have one problem though, you know."

"We do? Wait. What are you talking about?"

I rise up, perversely enjoying the hint of panic I hear in his voice. "It's just that you're too good at what you do."

I watch as his face relaxes as he realizes he's being teased. "Is that so?"

"You caught my stalker without having to take me back to The Firehouse."

"I see. And that's a problem?"

"Not if you promise to take me back."

His grin is pure, carnal wickedness. "Sweetheart," he says as he carefully curls up next to me. "I'll buy us a membership in the morning."

Epilogue

I wake to the sun streaming in through the windows of Riley's Malibu house. He says his love-hate relationship with Los Angeles is all over, and that he only bought property in Malibu because he wanted beach access, but I know better. After all, as Ian Taggart told me when he was in town last month, Riley knows perfectly well that Malibu isn't really Los Angeles.

I smile at the memory, because that was also the day when Ian told Riley that he was off the books of McKay-Taggart for the next four months, freeing Riley's schedule for another consulting gig—this time for *Her Secret Service*, Lyle's next movie based on Serena Dean-Miles' erotic thriller.

I roll over, enjoying the feel of the cool sheets against my naked skin as I think about all the wonderful perks that consulting job will bestow on me. Then I frown, realizing that cool sheets mean that I'm alone in bed—and have been for a while.

"Hey, beautiful."

Riley's voice caresses me, as smooth as whiskey and just as intoxicating. I prop myself up on my elbows and raise my brows. "You want to explain to me why, on the first day of my two-week vacation, I wake up alone in bed?"

"Might be because I had to feed your cat." He takes a step toward me. "Or it might be because I had to answer the door. A delivery man brought this." He passes me a letter-sized brown envelope.

I sit up, confused, pulling the sheet around me for warmth more than modesty. The windows are open and the breeze off the Pacific is cool. "What is it?"

"Open it."

The envelope is closed only with a clasp, so it's easy enough to get inside. I turn it over and a plane ticket falls into my lap. Confused, I read the destination, then frown as a slow anger starts to boil inside me.

"That lousy prick," I say. "Taggart said he wasn't going to offer you any more freelance work for four full months so that you could concentrate on Lyle and Serena's movie."

"Yeah, but that gig doesn't start for another three weeks. This trip is only for ten days."

"Ten days in China starting tomorrow," I say after another glance at the ticket. "Dammit, Riley, this trip is over my vacation." I will myself not to cry, but all I want to do is burst into tears. I haven't taken a vacation in forever and I only took time off now because Riley specifically told me he wanted to spend it together.

"Huh," he says, his brow furrowed as he takes the ticket from me. He turns it sideways, narrows his eyes, then steps back and says, "Oh! Of course."

"What?" I demand, confusion piling on top of my irritation.

"You need this, too." He reaches into his back pocket and pulls out a small, flat box. Like a jewelry store might use for a bracelet. I open it, then see another ticket folded up on top. I smirk, then pull it out, laughing when I see my name on it.

"Not a mission," I say, rising to put my arms around him. "A vacation for two."

"That's not exactly accurate," he says, and if it weren't for the twinkle in those dark, dreamy eyes, I'd be worried all over again. Instead, I'm intrigued.

I take a step back. "Okay," I demand. "What have I got wrong?"

"Anything else in that box?"

I shoot him one suspicious glance, then poke at the pad of cotton on which the folded ticket had been sitting. My finger hits something hard, and I immediately lift my head, looking once again at Riley, who looks incredibly pleased with himself.

I pull off the cotton to reveal a platinum ring with a stunning diamond, its facets catching the morning light and gleaming like starlight.

My legs go weak, and I fall back onto the bed at the same time that Riley drops to one knee in front of me. "Not a vacation. A honeymoon."

"A honeymoon," I repeat.

"We can stop in Vegas on the way. Or we can break convention and do the honeymoon first."

My lips twitch. "Aren't you jumping the gun a little?"

He flashes me a wide, sexy smile that's just a little sheepish. "Natasha Black," he says, taking the ring from my palm. "Will you marry me?"

I laugh with delight, and I'm pretty sure my heart has skipped a beat or two. "Yes," I say. "Oh, yes, Riley. Of course, yes."

He slides the ring onto my finger, then kisses me in a way that makes clear I belong to him. As if I had any doubt at all.

When we break apart, I sigh happily then tug his hand so that we both drop down to sit on the edge of the bed. "Why China?" I ask as I gaze into the fire of my engagement ring.

"I wanted to go someplace exotic," he says. "And where we could get completely lost together. What better place than somewhere we don't speak the language?" His brow furrows. "You don't speak Chinese, do you?"

I laugh. "No. And if the idea is to get lost with you, I have absolutely no motivation to learn it."

"Good." He brushes a strand of hair off my face. "Shame on you for thinking I'd leave you alone on your vacation." Mischief twinkles in his eyes. "I really should punish you for that."

"Absolutely you should," I say, pulling him down on top of me. "Spank me. Tease me. Punish me. And then make love to me. Slowly, please. And very thoroughly."

"Sweetheart, I can't think of anything I'd rather do." He cups my face and looks into my eyes with so much intensity I almost can't bear the passion I see there. "Nothing except marry you, and I'm already planning to do that soon."

"Yes," I say, hooking an arm around his neck and pulling him close, craving the feel of him against me, inside me. "Yes," I repeat before I lose myself in the magic of his touch. "You absolutely are."

THE END

I'm so grateful to Lexi Blake for letting my play in the world of McKay-Taggart, and I was sold on the concept from the moment Lexi told me about her vision of a superhero universe, where characters from one world crossover into another. I've always known Lexi was freaking brilliant, and I think this project just sealed the deal for me. Not to mention the bonus of being part of a collection with some of my favorite authors and friends!

I love Riley and Natasha, and have since the moment they popped onto the page in *Wicked Dirty*. I hope you love them, too!

XXOO
JK

Sign up for the 1001 Dark Nights Newsletter
and be entered to win a Tiffany Lock necklace.

There's a contest every quarter!

Go to www.1001DarkNights.com to subscribe.

As a bonus, all subscribers will receive a free copy of
Discovery Bundle Three
Featuring stories by
Sidney Bristol, Darcy Burke, T. Gephart
Stacey Kennedy, Adriana Locke
JB Salsbury, and Erika Wilde

Discover the Lexi Blake Crossover Collection
Available now!

Close Cover by Lexi Blake

Remy Guidry doesn't do relationships. He tried the marriage thing once, back in Louisiana, and learned the hard way that all he really needs in life is a cold beer, some good friends, and the occasional hookup. His job as a bodyguard with McKay-Taggart gives him purpose and lovely perks, like access to Sanctum. The last thing he needs in his life is a woman with stars in her eyes and babies in her future.

Lisa Daley's life is going in the right direction. She has graduated from college after years of putting herself through school. She's got a new job at an accounting firm and she's finished her Sanctum training. Finally on her own and having fun, her life seems pretty perfect. Except she's lonely and the one man she wants won't give her a second look.

There is one other little glitch. Apparently, her new firm is really a front for the mob and now they want her dead. Assassins can really ruin a fun girls' night out. Suddenly strapped to the very same six-foot-five-inch hunk of a bodyguard who makes her heart pound, Lisa can't decide if this situation is a blessing or a curse.

As the mob closes in, Remy takes his tempting new charge back to the safest place he knows—his home in the bayou. Surrounded by his past, he can't help wondering if Lisa is his future. To answer that question, he just has to keep her alive.

* * * *

Her Guardian Angel by Larissa Ione

After a difficult childhood and a turbulent stint in the military, Declan Burke finally got his act together. Now he's a battle-hardened professional bodyguard who takes his job at McKay-Taggart seriously and his playtime – and his play*mates* – just as seriously. One thing he never does, however, is mix business with pleasure. But when the mysterious, gorgeous Suzanne D'Angelo needs his protection from a stalker, his desire for her burns out of control, tempting him to break all the rules...even as he's drawn into a dark, dangerous world he didn't know existed.

Suzanne is an earthbound angel on her critical first mission: protecting Declan from an emerging supernatural threat at all costs. To keep him close, she hires him as her bodyguard. It doesn't take long for her to realize that she's in over her head, defenseless against this devastatingly sexy human who makes her crave his forbidden touch.

Together they'll have to draw on every ounce of their collective training to resist each other as the enemy closes in, but soon it becomes apparent that nothing could have prepared them for the menace to their lives…or their hearts.

* * * *

Justify Me by J. Kenner

McKay-Taggart operative Riley Blade has no intention of returning to Los Angeles after his brief stint as a consultant on mega-star Lyle Tarpin's latest action flick. Not even for Natasha Black, Tarpin's sexy personal assistant who'd gotten under his skin. Why would he, when Tasha made it absolutely clear that—attraction or not—she wasn't interested in a fling, much less a relationship.

But when Riley learns that someone is stalking her, he races to her side. Determined to not only protect her, but to convince her that—no matter what has hurt her in the past—he's not only going to fight for her, he's going to win her heart. Forever.

* * * *

Say You Won't Let Go by Corinne Michaels

I've had two goals my entire life:
1. Make it big in country music.
2. Get the hell out of Bell Buckle.

I was doing it. I was on my way, until Cooper Townsend landed backstage at my show in Dallas.

This gorgeous, rugged, man of few words was one cowboy I couldn't afford to let distract me. But with his slow smile and rough hands, I just couldn't keep away.

Now, there are outside forces conspiring against us. Maybe we should've known better? Maybe not. Even with the protection from Wade Rycroft, bodyguard for McKay-Taggart, I still don't feel safe. I won't let him get hurt because of me. All I know is that I want to hold on, but know the right thing to do is to let go...

* * * *

His to Protect by Carly Phillips

Talia Shaw has spent her adult life working as a scientist for a big pharmaceutical company. She's focused on saving lives, not living life. When her lab is broken into and it's clear someone is after the top secret formula she's working on, she turns to the one man she can trust. The same irresistible man she turned away years earlier because she was too young and naive to believe a sexy guy like Shane Landon could want *her*.

Shane Landon's bodyguard work for McKay-Taggart is the one thing that brings him satisfaction in his life. Relationships come in second to the job. Always. Then little brainiac Talia Shaw shows up in his backyard, frightened and on the run, and his world is turned upside down. And not just because she's found him naked in his outdoor shower, either.

With Talia's life in danger, Shane has to get her out of town and to her eccentric, hermit mentor who has the final piece of the formula she's been working on, while keeping her safe from the men who are after her. Guarding Talia's body certainly isn't any hardship, but he never expects to fall hard and fast for his best friend's little sister and the only woman who's ever really gotten under his skin.

* * * *

Rescuing Sadie by Susan Stoker

Sadie Jennings was used to being protected. As the niece of Sean Taggart, and the receptionist at McKay-Taggart Group, she was constantly surrounded by Alpha men more than capable, and willing, to lay down their life for her. But when she visits her friend in San

Antonio, and acts on suspicious activity at Milena's workplace, Sadie puts both of them in the crosshairs of a madman. After several harrowing weeks, her friend is now safe, but for Sadie, the repercussions of her rash act linger on.

Chase Jackson, no stranger to dangerous situations as a captain in the US Army, has volunteered himself as Sadie's bodyguard. He fell head over heels for the beautiful woman the first time he laid eyes on her. With a Delta Force team at his back, he reassures the Taggart's that Sadie will be safe. But when the situation in San Antonio catches up with her, Chase has to use everything he's learned over his career to keep his promise...and to keep Sadie alive long enough to officially make her his.

About J. Kenner

J. Kenner (aka Julie Kenner) is the *New York Times, USA Today, Publishers Weekly, Wall Street Journal* and #1 International bestselling author of over one-hundred novels, novellas and short stories in a variety of genres.

JK has been praised by *Publishers Weekly* as an author with a "flair for dialogue and eccentric characterizations" and by *RT Bookclub* for having "cornered the market on sinfully attractive, dominant antiheroes and the women who swoon for them." A five-time finalist for Romance Writers of America's prestigious RITA award, JK took home the first RITA trophy awarded in the category of erotic romance in 2014 for her novel, *Claim Me* (book 2 of her Stark Trilogy).

In her previous career as an attorney, JK worked as a lawyer in Southern California and Texas. She currently lives in Central Texas, with her husband, two daughters, and two rather spastic cats.

Visit JK online at www.jkenner.com
Subscribe to JK's Newsletter
Text JKenner to 21000 to subscribe to JK's text alerts
Twitter
Instagram
Facebook Page
Facebook Fan Group

Tame Me
A Stark International Novella
By J. Kenner

Aspiring actress Jamie Archer is on the run. From herself. From her wild child ways. From the screwed up life that she left behind in Los Angeles. And, most of all, from Ryan Hunter—the first man who has the potential to break through her defenses to see the dark fears and secrets she hides.

Stark International Security Chief Ryan Hunter knows only one thing for sure—he wants Jamie. Wants to hold her, make love to her, possess her, and claim her. Wants to do whatever it takes to make her his.

But after one night of bliss, Jamie bolts. And now it's up to Ryan to not only bring her back, but to convince her that she's running away from the best thing that ever happened to her—*him*.

* * * *

That, I think, *was one hell of a party.*

I am standing with my back to the Pacific as I watch the efficient crew break down the lovely white tents. The leftover food has already been packed away. The trash has been discarded. The band left hours ago, and the last of the guests have already departed.

Even the paparazzi who had camped out on the beach hoping to snag a few choice pictures of my best friend Nikki Fairchild's wedding to multi-bazillionaire and former tennis star Damien Stark are long gone.

I sigh and tell myself that this vague emptiness I'm feeling isn't melancholy. Instead, it's an aftereffect of staying up all night drinking and partying. I am, of course, lying. I'm melancholy as shit, but I figure that's normal. After all, I've just watched my best friend get married to the one man in the entire universe who is absolutely, positively perfect for her. Great news, and I'm really and truly happy for her, but she found him without trolling through the entire male population of Los Angeles.

Compare that to me, who's fucked approximately eighty percent of that population and still hasn't found a guy like Damien, and I think it's safe to say that Nikki got the last decent man.

Okay, maybe not the last one, I amend as I catch sight of Ryan Hunter coming down the walking path that winds from Damien's Malibu house all the way to the beach where I'm now standing. Ryan is the Chief of Security for Stark International, and he and I have been the *de facto* host and hostess for this post-wedding soiree ever since the bride and groom took off in a helicopter bound for marital bliss.

Ryan is not among the eighty-percent, and that is truly a shame. The man is seriously hot, with piercing blue eyes and chestnut hair worn in a short, almost military style that accents the hard lines and angles of his face. He's tall and lean, but strong and sexy. I've seen him now in both jeans and a tux, and the curve of his ass alone is enough to make a woman drool.

We've gotten to know each other over the last few months, and I consider him a friend. Frankly, I'd like to consider him more, and I think he feels the same, even though he has yet to make a move.

I've seen the way he watches me, the heat that flares in his eyes when he thinks I'm not looking. Maybe he's shy—but I doubt it. He's got a dangerous edge that perfectly suits his job as the head security dude for a guy like Damien and an enterprise like Stark International.

Nikki once told me that there was nothing Ryan liked better than chasing monsters. I believe it, and as I watch him stride down the walking path, his movements a combination of grace and power, I can imagine him in battle and am certain that he would do whatever it takes to win.

No, I don't believe that Ryan Hunter is shy. All I know is that he's never made a move on me, and that's a damn shame.

And now, of course, it's too late. Because I'm heading back home to Texas tomorrow as part of my newly implemented life goal of getting my shit together. And, as part of the whole Repair My Life plan, I've put the kibosh on sleeping around. I'm focusing on Jamie Archer. On figuring out who she is and what she wants, and step one of The Plan is to not do the nasty with every hot guy who crosses my path.

Honestly, men are so five minutes ago.

So far, The Plan is going pretty good. I found a tenant for my Studio City condo a few months ago, then went home to live with my parents in Dallas. It's hard being a twenty-five-year-old actress in Los Angeles, especially one who has yet to land a decent gig. There are too many guys who are prettier than me—and who know it. And way too many opportunities for a fast fuck.

Texas is slower. Easier. And even though it's hardly the acting capital of the universe, I've already had a few auditions, and I think I may even have a decent shot for a job as an on-air reporter at a local affiliate. I'd auditioned right before flying out here for the wedding, and I'm hoping to hear back from the programming director any day now.

And, yes, true, I'd also auditioned for a commercial here in SoCal, but I didn't get the job. I tell myself that's a good thing because I would have taken it and stayed in Los Angeles, because I love Los Angeles and my friends are here. But that would have put me right back on that hamster wheel of auditioning and fucking, and then starting the whole destructive process right over again.

The Plan is good, I tell myself as I watch the crew finish the job. The Plan is wise.

As a dozen workmen haul the last of the tent poles to a nearby truck, the supervisor approaches me with a clipboard and a pen. He takes me through the list, and I duly check off all the various items, confirming that the final details have been attended to.

Then I sign the form, thank him, and watch as he climbs into the truck and drives away.

"So that's it," Ryan says as he approaches me. He's still in tuxedo pants and the starched white shirt, but the cummerbund is gone, as is the jacket. He really does look sexy as hell, but it's his bare feet that have done me in. There's something so damn devil-may-care about a guy in a tux barefoot on the beach, and I can't help but wonder if there really is a bit of the devil in Ryan Hunter.

And if there is, will I ever get to peek at the wickedness?

"No more cars in the driveway," he continues, as I try to yank my thoughts back to reality. "And I just signed the invoice for the car park company. I think we can safely call this thing a wrap. And a success." His smile is slow and easy and undeniably sexy. "It really was one hell of a party."

I laugh. "I was just thinking the same thing." My stomach does a little twisting number, and I tell myself it's hunger. After all, champagne isn't that filling, and I'm sure all the dancing I did during the night burned off the three slices of wedding cake I'd devoured.

I'm lying again, of course. It's not hunger that's making my stomach flutter. It's Ryan. And as I stand there silently wishing he'd just touch me already, I'm also getting more and more irritated. Because why the hell *hasn't* he touched me already? We've spent time together. We've even danced together during various club outings with friends. Not touching, maybe, but close enough that the air between us was thick with promise.

And once, when Damien had a security scare, he sent Ryan to check on me. I'd been wearing a tiny bikini with a sheer cover-up, and I looked damn hot. But he hadn't made a move. We'd ended up talking for hours, which was great, and I even made him eggs, which is about as domesticated as I get.

I'm certain I haven't been imagining that sizzle between us—and yet never once has he made a move. I can't fathom why, and the whole situation grates on me.

Except I'm not supposed to care—Ryan is not part of The Plan.

On behalf of 1001 Dark Nights,

Liz Berry and M.J. Rose would like to thank ~

Steve Berry
Doug Scofield
Kim Guidroz
Jillian Stein
InkSlinger PR
Dan Slater
Asha Hossain
Chris Graham
Fedora Chen
Kasi Alexander
Jessica Johns
Dylan Stockton
Richard Blake
BookTrib After Dark
and Simon Lipskar